"Zoe, you okay in there?"

"Yes. Come in. I'm just finishing up."

Ben walked in. "You're determined to tame your hair. Leave it alone. It's pretty down."

"It's a squirrel's tail. I need another band," she said, unable to find the one she'd had before.

Seeing it on the floor, she picked it up and snapped it around the ends, when Ben caught her around the waist.

"Just what do you think you're doing?" she whispered.

"Collecting on a piece of my debt." He leaned against the sink and brought her against him.

"That's unfair, Ben." She lost her grip on her hair and the band spiraled off, falling onto the floor again. "You made the rule of no fooling around while we're working together."

"I love that you have such a good memory. But if you remember correctly, our business concluded with the arrest. We declared the case closed."

Books by Carmen Green

Kimani Romance

This Time for Good
The Perfect Solitaire

CARMEN GREEN

National bestselling author Carmen Green was born in Buffalo, New York, and had plans to study law before becoming a published author. While raising her three children, she wrote her first book on legal pads and transcribed it onto a computer on weekends. She sold her first novel in 1993. Since that time she has written and published more than thirty novels and novellas, and is proud that one of her books, *Commitments,* was made into a TV movie in 2001. In *Commitments,* Carmen even had a cameo role.

In addition to writing full-time, Carmen is now a mom of four, and has just completed her master's degree in creative writing. She's a founding member of the Femme Fantastik Tour, a group that tours military bases promoting their literary works throughout the United States and Europe. In her spare time, Carmen likes live music, gardening, vacations in quiet, tropical places and long cruises that don't require her to do anything but read, sleep and eat. Her next novel for Kimani Romance, *Sensual Winds,* will be available in July 2009. You can contact Carmen at www.carmengreen.blogspot.com or carmengreen1201@yahoo.com.

The
Perfect
Solitaire

Carmen Green

KIMANI™
ROMANCE

Danielle Alexandria Green
You're such a blessing to my life.
I'll always love you.
To the Sparrow. You are always with me.

KIMANI PRESS™

ISBN-13: 978-0-373-86118-7

PLEASE RECYCLE

Recycling programs
for this product may
not exist in your area.

THE PERFECT SOLITAIRE

www.kimanipress.com

Printed in U.S.A.

Dear Reader,

I'd like to introduce you to the Hoods. They're a wonderful family of handsome, intelligent and sexy men who are on the right side of wrong, and who practice their own brand of street justice against those who've slipped through the loopholes of the legal system. My Hood family give their own special twist to the infamous fairy tale *Robin Hood.* I hope you enjoy reading about them as much as I enjoyed creating them. The first book is Ben's story, but later you'll meet his twin, Rob, and then Zachary. I assure you that the women in their lives love these men, and I hope you will, too. Please be sure to drop me a note at carmengreen1201@yahoo.com. You can also keep up to date on the happenings in my world by visiting my blog at www.carmengreen.blogspot.com.

Many blessings,

Carmen

Chapter 1

Zoe lay on her back in the center of his bed, as Ben Hood teased her womanhood with the sixteen-inch strand of multi-colored Tahitian pearls she'd borrowed from her jewelry store for the White Linen Party. He smelled of man and cologne, and coupled with the yearning in his eyes, she couldn't resist him any longer. Her nipples were like radar beams pointing right at his chest. And it seemed, under their own volition, that the hardened tips lifted her thirty-year-old body, and her arms circled his neck.

The room was bathed in candlelight, yet she could still see his triumphant smile. "I thought you could resist me?" he teased, his knees dropping to her sides, his arms circling her back as he pulled the black bra off. His left hand palmed her breast before his luscious lips covered the caramel-colored tip.

"You're too hard to resist." A low guttural moan tore from her throat as he ravaged one breast then the other. She shook with wanting. "Oh, goodness," she moaned, and he laughed deep in his chest, his hand straying down between her legs. There was this direct connection between her breasts and her essence, and she'd never met a man who knew how to make them work together like him.

"Who knew I would meet someone as fine as you at a *conference?*" Zoe laughed. Ben chuckled.

His hands moved over her body as if he'd known her for years, yet this was their first time. Still, the shyness she usually felt was gone. Stripped bare, he rolled onto his back pulling her on top of him, his lips never leaving her breasts. She loved the way he appreciated them, as if there was some type of life substance coming from them. She felt the tugging inside, the warmth of sexual desire filling her, making her want him to have her in any way he wanted.

Ben released her breast and looked into her eyes. She descended for a kiss, his mouth claiming hers. The word carnal came to mind. Dizzying and potent, his tongue sought hers and she met him with a passion she hadn't felt in a long time. This was what she'd been wanting for so long, and had been missing in relationships in her twenties. At thirty-five, Ben was a man. A *real* man. There was no escaping that fact, and the way he wanted her, the way his hands held her against his sex and his mouth claimed hers, well, she was nearly ready to come right then. She grabbed his chin, his day-long growth of beard tantalizing her palm.

"Yeah, baby? What you want?" He caught his bottom lip between his teeth and gave her a look so sexy, her heart skipped a beat. Having him ask as his hands played the guessing game between her legs with her pearls was sexy as hell. She sucked in her breath and nodded when he guessed just right. His thumb glided over the heart of her sexuality and she pushed against him.

"You're gorgeous. You know that?" he asked. His gaze roamed her as he caressed her most intimate parts.

She smiled down at him. "You're biased." She stuck out her tongue and he was up in a flash and had captured it between his lips. They were again chest to chest, sex to sex, and she had to have him.

Zoe wrapped her legs around his back and pushed, and he shook his head and murmured, "No." "Why?" she whispered, nipping his ear, backing up a little. She reached down and took him in her hands.

He muttered an expletive as he watched her and she wrinkled her nose at him, laughing. "Aren't you about to do that?" she teased.

"Woman, don't play. That's a dangerous weapon. Handle with care." Even as he taunted and teased her, his hands never left her body. His strokes were purposeful and strong. She felt wanted. Needed, even.

Carefully, she wound the pearls around his sex and rolled them gently up and down. His eyes widened. "You were telling me why I couldn't have this," she said, and kissed his manhood. His thigh muscles flexed. The stimulation from the pearls and her mouth seemed to drive him close to the edge, and his chest rose and fell in quick pants.

"You keep that up and I won't be able to please you," he said.

"Yes, you will." With each stroke and suck, he drove his hands through her hair until he couldn't take any more. He pulled her up and took the pearls from her hands. "You're dangerous with these, you know that?" She smiled, biting his chin. "You're a bad girl, Zoe."

"I want you," she told him as she touched his hardened sex again, her legs tingling. Zoe was surprised at her confession. She'd never spoken those words to another man in her life. She wondered how she'd feel in the morning, but she didn't care right now. She wanted him and she meant to have him.

Opening for him, she lifted her legs and he kissed her as he pushed inside. They both smiled. She, in surprise. He, in knowing. "Big," she whispered.

"You can handle me, baby," he said, and began to move in her.

Each stroke made up for all she'd missed.

"You're gorgeous," he whispered, again and again. Her desire soared the more they moved as one. His thrusts were powerful, his six pack of tight muscles a visual delight. But it was his eyes glazed in pleasure that drove her closer to the finish line. Watching their bodies meet in carnal bliss, the way his hands took possession of her thighs and bring about her climax made her arch, her fingers running up his arms. She wanted to hold him to her, but she didn't want to say that. The end was approaching fast and Ben seemed to know.

"Come here," he said and lifted her, their bodies still joined. He seemed to innately know that this was the only time she'd completely let go. He moved inside of her to a place no man had been before, and she cried out her climax, her body clutching his, words falling from her lips she couldn't explain or remember. A second later he pulsed inside of her, their mouths attached, their mating finally at a blissful end.

Their breath wasn't fully recovered when his phone began

to ring. Neither of them moved; her head on his shoulder, his muscular arms cradling her. It rang again and stopped, then started again. "That's the signal. I have to get it."

"What signal?" Zoe asked as he lay her down on the bed, leaned over and grabbed his pants.

"The phone rang three separate times in succession. That means pick up. It's probably Rob."

"Who's Rob?" Zoe rolled onto her side, wanting Ben's attention back on her.

"My twin brother." Ben smiled and dragged a curl of her hair down to her breast. It popped back into place. Zoe nuzzled Ben's chin, half listening as he talked. She recalled now that he'd mentioned that he was a twin and Rob was older by four minutes.

"Rob? What's going on? Yeah. Where's Zach? I'm off tonight and I've got company." The sensual glow cleared from his eyes, and the finger he'd been using to run down the center of her chest was now turning on the lamplight.

"We can pick up Pickens tomorrow," Ben said.

"The warrant is still good. No, if you need me, I guess I can come. What else? I have company, Rob."

Warrant? Hadn't he said he was an investigator? Not a bounty hunter. Those were two distinctly different things.

Zoe gathered her G-string and snapped it into place, frantically searching for her bra. Skipping it, she put on the white-linen dress she'd worn to the party. It was very wrinkled, but linen was that kind of material. She stepped into it, hating she couldn't find her bra. Her nipples were chafing against the material. How could she have been so wrong? Wild passion was a terrible thing and had clouded her good sense.

She quickly snapped up all of her belongings and went around to the side of the bed so Ben could see her. "I'll call you tomorrow," she said, and he half stood, but she waved him down. "I can find my way out."

"You don't have to leave." He looked confused, and regret passed over his face.

"No. I'm gone," she told him.

Her shoes tapped against the marble floors decisively. Though not a cop, all she could remember from childhood was her mother and the nervous way she'd approached the door every time the doorbell rang when Zoe's dad had been at work. She'd been waiting for bad news and now she'd finally gotten it. Two months ago, her father had been left for dead in a hit-and-run accident in the line of duty, and because of budget constraints by the city, medical benefits he needed were being cut. Her mother was barely supporting them on her teacher's salary. No way. Investigator. Cop. It didn't matter. She would not be her mother.

Just reading Zoe McKnight's name in the e-mail made Ben Hood's thigh muscles stretch and his biceps flex in remembrance of how good their lovemaking had been.

Three months had passed since she'd been right here in his house, and he should have forgotten her by now, but he hadn't. Nat King Cole was right. She was unforgettable.

Zoe was far more beautiful than the movie stars or the women music videos touted as icons of beauty. She was an authentic woman with a soft stomach he'd enjoyed holding in his hands, shapely breasts that filled his palms, and thighs that gripped his in earnest. And that unruly mass of hair that she tried to tame with a headband or clips, and that he could never forget pulling free and letting go wild.

Her smile still lit up his mind. *"I've got to go. I'll call you tomorrow."* Those were her last words to him over three months ago. He'd been a one-night piece of ass, and that didn't sit well with him. How many times in his younger, stupider days had he promised to call a woman and hadn't?

Karma was a mean old bitch.

He tapped the keyboard and paged through the e-mail file, reading why she wanted to hire Hood Investigations, Inc.

Her jewelry stores, Zoe's Diamonds on Peachtree and Zoe's Diamonds at the Galleria, kept getting robbed. The amounts taken weren't large and his initial thought was that it was an inside job, but instinct told him Zoe wouldn't have pursued their company if she hadn't already considered that possibility.

Atlanta stores and gas stations had been plagued with smash-and-grab type robberies with thieves stealing ATM machines. But these robberies were different. These were smooth break-ins and they were affecting Zoe's economic future.

The stores had been fit with sensors and cameras by a reputable security company, but they'd been disabled every single time. So far, only merchandise had been taken, but Zoe was worried that the thieves were becoming more brazen and striking more often, and soon, somebody might get hurt. Her biggest concern was that she was planning a multi-million-dollar expansion project and not only did she need A-1 credit, but a low-incidence crime rating.

It's an inside job, Zoe, baby. Saying her name made him want her again in the same way he craved sweets the year he'd given them up.

Shaking images of her from his mind, Ben reviewed the remainder of the e-mail files he needed to send back to Rob, the president of Hood I.N.V., and responded about two other cases that weren't closed yet. His sister, who owned her own cleaning company, knocked on his office door.

"Come in, Mel."

"Ben, I'm about to head down to Rob's house, but I found something interesting behind your nightstand."

He swung around in his chair. "What are you doing behind my nightstand? Didn't you just have surgery on your rotator cuff six weeks ago?"

Mel, the baby of the family of five, was a hard worker, supporting her hearing-impaired daughter and her six-year-old all on her own. "I wasn't lifting anything." Her compact size fooled many people, but not her brothers and sister who knew of her black belts in Aikido and Hapkido. "I found these fancy pearls when I was dusting, and I couldn't help but think you might want to give them back, or I can take them home and consider them an early bonus."

Ben was out of his chair in a slow movement. The fun he'd had with Zoe and these pearls brought back fond memories. "You may clean behind my nightstand anytime. Thanks, sis. Your bonus is in the mail."

She laughed as he popped a kiss onto her forehead. "Tahitian pearls. Nice."

Ben relieved Mel of the fancy baubles. "How do you know they're Tahitian?"

"I have a deep appreciation for fine jewelry." She touched his chin. "That look says that you should return them. She must be pretty special."

"Very much so." Ben walked his sister to her car. The sun warmed his skin and he had the feeling the day was only going to get better.

"Approach her as if she's a case. Carefully and with a lot of passion. You'll get her."

Ben saw his sister off and studied the pearls before deciding what he wanted. He'd return the pearls. The same way he'd gotten them. He'd seduce Zoe, just like he had three months ago. And he'd start by finding out who was trying to ruin her business.

Chapter 2

"Why not hire a twenty-four-hour guard service, Zoe? I don't think you need to get some expensive investigation company to charge a whole lot of money to come in and solve a petty theft problem."

At the store, Zoe locked the safe that held loose diamonds, and other precious stones. She turned around and looked at her older sister, Faye, who'd been hovering for the better part of an hour. "I don't want guards sitting in my stores. None of the other stores have them, and I'm afraid they'll turn off customers."

She straightened the clingy fuchsia dress over her curves—fuchsia being the signature color of Zoe's Diamonds on Peachtree—and checked her makeup one last time.

The past two months had been tough with her stores having been robbed three times. She couldn't believe she'd been targeted after all the security measures she'd taken.

When Zoe turned around, Faye held a long strand of silver pearls in one hand and a gold rope necklace in the other. Zoe chose the pearls. Similar to the ones she'd worn the evening she'd spent at Ben's, but not nearly as expensive. That night had cost her emotionally and financially. From the moment she'd met Ben, she'd been attracted to him. She liked his talk of his big family and the crazy antics of his two brothers from when they were boys. He'd even confided, after some probing, that he'd wanted children.

Zoe had been impressed. She only had one sister, but she and Faye didn't see eye-to-eye on much, and having another sibling might have helped them bond better as children. But his being an investigator was a turn off, despite his good looks, his ability to hold a stimulating conversation and his limitless talent in bed.

But her biggest regret of the evening was that she'd lost the ten-thousand-dollar strand of Tahitian pearls. She'd never found them, and as much as she'd thought of calling Ben to ask if she'd dropped them, she'd never completely found the nerve.

Zoe took the strand of freshwater pearls her sister offered, and wrapped her neck with them twice, making a choker. She completed the look with an amethyst cuff bracelet and a thin amethyst anklet that accented her high heels. She was ready.

"What now?" Zoe asked Faye while she pulled back her hair, wishing she'd straightened the wild curls.

"You don't need Hood. They're too expensive."

"They get results and that's all I care about. I'm ready to move on to the next phase of my life. When I stopped paying Charles spousal support two years ago, I said I wasn't ever going to get married again. I saved all that money and it's getting invested in my dream, Faye. Zoe's

Diamonds on Peachtree is my dream. Nobody has the right to steal that from me."

"I know, but giving the money to Hood is the same thing as giving it to Charles."

"How do you figure that? If you're still arguing Charles' side of the divorce four years after the ink dried, you may as well leave now."

So many unsaid words hung between them. There had always been jealousy between her and Faye for years. Faye had grown up falsely believing that Zoe had somehow gotten more out of life than she had. Though Faye was five years older and had taken the lion's share of college-fund money their parents had saved, Faye still made snide comments about Zoe getting to go to the school of her choice. She didn't bother to mention that Zoe had gone on scholarships with little assistance from their parents.

"Zoe, I don't know why you still think I'm on Charles' side."

"I know what I saw which was you and Flint move into my house with my ex after he and I broke up. I saw you and Flint and Charles' new woman become virtually best friends when I could have used a sister to comfort me. You brought her to the same salon I got my hair done at, our church here in Atlanta, even my favorite dinner spots when you were visiting Mom and Dad. If you weren't trying to rub it in my face that you were Charles' lady's best friend, I don't know what else to call it."

Faye looked humiliated and embarrassed. "Okay, Zoe. At the time, I wasn't a VP at the bank, I was just a manager. Flint had gotten laid off so things were getting tight. You'd always had the best and I wanted to see how the other half lived. I got carried away," Fay offered with a shrug. "I shouldn't have forgotten that blood is thicker than water."

Anger pulsed through Zoe's veins. She was surprised that her feelings were still so strong. "Why'd you come down here, Faye? This is the last day of your vacation, and you're here in the store with me. I've got an appointment. Why don't you go spend your last day in Atlanta with Mom and Dad?"

"Because I just want it to be us girls. I do have a lot to atone for." Faye looked like she wanted to cry, and Zoe didn't want to deal with her emotions today. "I just thought we could recapture some of the days of our youth. We weren't always fighting." She laughed and it sounded like a sob. "I see how wrong I was now that Flint and I are getting divorced. I empathize with you."

Zoe had felt betrayed by her sister and she wasn't sure there was a way to recapture the days they had gotten along when they were young. "The thing about that kind of hurt, Faye, is that it doesn't come with an expiration date. Family is supposed to stick together, and I couldn't tell you then and I can't tell you now who to be friends with. So, if you'll excuse me, I've got work to do."

"So you're dismissing me?" Faye no longer sounded sincere, but hard, and Zoe wasn't intimidated by her older sister anymore.

"It took you years to say those words to me. I need more than three minutes to process them. What brought about this change of heart, Faye?"

"It's just time to bury the hatchet. I mean—" she chuckled hard. "I really do need a break from all the stress of my divorce. Maybe when this is over, you can treat me to a sister weekend away to Savannah or something."

The real Faye had finally shown up. Her weak attempt at an apology was really the well-crafted pitch for a free vacation. Faye's sour face and her woe-is-me attitude only served as a reminder of her constant defection to the Nathanson side of the road, and Zoe was short on sorrow.

"I've got work to do. I'm sure Daddy needs you to do something for him at the house. Why don't you go over there and help him with his exercises?"

Faye scoffed. "He needs a physical therapist, not a daughter."

"That would be me the evenings I don't work, and Mom when she's not teaching. But since you're here you can pitch in."

Zoe left the stockroom, heading to the front of the store spraying each display case with special cleaner so that they gleamed after she wiped them. She intentionally left a cloth to see if her sister would get to work. Faye neglectfully dragged her finger along the glass and pouted as she followed Zoe.

"It's just one more day," Faye said in her own defense. "Besides, I'd rather be with you. I'm more accustomed to dressing up for work at the bank than dressing down to help Dad stretch, and I can meet handsome single men, right?"

"Yes, they come in here to shop for their fiancés. Would you stop with the finger? I just cleaned the glass. Get that cloth and wipe off all those cases, Faye. You're making double work for me. I'll be back."

Zoe paced the small stockroom, stretching her tense neck muscles. She touched every drawer, making sure all were closed that held plastic and velvet bags of earrings, bracelets and necklaces.

If she stopped moving, she might tell Faye she'd all but written her off. Zoe stopped herself from saying the words and tried to center herself. She had a job to do and that didn't involve Faye.

"All done." Faye popped in back without the cloth.

"I'm going with Hood. If you want to help me, stay here with Ireland while she opens the store. Be an extra pair of eyes and ears. Make sure nothing happens. When I come back, we'll have lunch and really talk this out."

She threw out the conciliatory bone, hoping her sister would decline. Truth be told, Zoe was tired of entertaining and paying for her assistant-vice-president-of-the-bank sister to eat out nearly every night.

Twice she'd asked Faye to pick up the check, but her cards had been declined. Though Zoe'd asked about Faye's money troubles, her sister had claimed her paycheck must not have been posted yet.

"Why waste the gas going back and forth when I can just go with you? Then after the meeting, we can eat." Faye looked around anxiously. "I can listen in on your meeting with the Hoods and be a second pair of eyes and ears. I've got lots of experience you don't give me credit for. I've sat in on security meetings at the highest levels, Zoe. I'm an officer at the bank in Greenville. I hold an extremely high security clearance. Possibly higher than your little security people." Faye took another look at Zoe's face and gave up. "I'll stay here."

Zoe left the store, relieved. She needed some peace from Faye's prying eyes and constant talking. She also needed to forgive her sister, she knew that, but not right now. Right now she needed a few minutes to compose her thoughts.

There was so much she wanted to say to Robinson Hood. She'd met him at a Young Entrepreneurs' luncheon of Atlanta three months ago, and had been impressed with his speech about the work he and his family did. Too bad. She'd done something she'd rarely done: gone back to a man's house.

Since then, she'd done her research and had found out

that Hood Investigations was revered by cops because they didn't have to play by cops' rules. Cops who would hire them if they had a problem. With that endorsement, she'd made the call.

Rob had set up the meeting right away.

Settling in her car, Zoe locked the doors and inhaled and exhaled the warm June air until her nerves no longer felt like the jumbled ball of rubber bands she kept in her office. She needed Hood to move fast and catch these people that were threatening her future. That's how she'd open. Then she'd outline the facts. She programmed the address into her GPS, and planned everything else she'd say all the way to the front door with the black block letters announcing Hood Investigations, Inc.

Opening the door, she walked inside. "I'm Zoe McKnight to see Rob Hood."

The male receptionist asked her to wait, and she soon saw Rob Hood.

"Good morning, Ms. McKnight. Rob Hood." He approached with a confident stride, his features prominent and chiseled like his brother's, yet slightly different from Ben's. The magnetism wasn't there. If she wasn't attracted to Rob Hood, she wouldn't be attracted to Ben, who was nearly Rob's spitting image.

"Pleased to meet you again. Please, call me Zoe."

"Zoe." Her head jerked involuntarily at the sound of his voice.

"Ben."

The strangest look appeared on Rob's face then his lips closed, he blinked and realization ignited the depths of his eyes. A half smile formed. "You've met my twin brother and business partner."

She'd met him on his bed just three months ago and had

let herself be taken to the stratosphere and back, yes. She'd been too high on lust to ever ask what he did for a living.

When he'd asked if she'd wanted a lick in the crease of her elbow, she'd moaned her consent. When he'd said to give it to him, she'd opened her whole body and given him a free pass to every pleasure zone, and each time he'd rung her bell, she'd hit the jackpot. There wasn't a night that had passed by when she didn't fantasize about making love to Ben. Sometimes she was the aggressor and other days he totally possessed her. Those nights, a cool shower was needed to cool her feminine energy.

Last week she'd broken down and gone to an adult store and bought a sex toy that she thought was close to his size and length. Zoe looked away from Ben, embarrassed. Yesterday she'd thrown it away. Nothing compared to the real thing, and now that she was looking at him, nothing ever would.

Maintaining her composure, she acknowledged him. "I remember your brother." She looked back at Ben and several curls came to rest against her MAC lip gloss. She slowly peeled the hair away from her mouth.

Ben sucked his teeth and muttered, "How well I remember."

She faltered, with Rob approaching from the right and Ben closing in from the left. Rob was a step ahead and her palm met his first. "Rob, I won't take up much of your time." She turned to Ben and couldn't quite meet his gaze. But she saw the pulse beating above the white collar of his shirt. Her tongue had been there.

"Zoe," Ben said. "Long time no hear." He made it sound as if each word weighed a hundred pounds.

He captured her left hand and held it, leaving it up to her to take it back. Damn him.

"Good to see you, too," she managed. "I'm here because I need your help, please. It shouldn't take too much time."

"Take as long as you need," Ben said. The same words had been issued that night, when she'd told him it took a long time for her to come.

Her legs seemed to have a mind of their own, but Zoe made herself stand still. The portfolio she'd been carrying slipped from her hand and papers scattered. Ben and Rob bent to retrieve them.

There was no denying it. The twins could pass for guards on any professional basketball team. They were tall, handsome, dark-skinned men with beautiful smiles, short haircuts and big hands.

The magic for Zoe had been in Ben's eyes. Almost as soon as she'd looked at him the night of the party, she'd known she would know him, and once she'd heard his voice and experienced his intelligence, she'd known she'd have him. The White Linen Party had been an auction and wine-tasting party designed to raise money for local animal shelters, and Ben had bid against her several times for exotic vacations. He'd gotten so bold, he'd come to stand beside her and bid. She'd found his boldness alluring and for the remainder of the night, he'd held her rapt attention. He'd won one vacation, she'd won one and he'd taken her home.

"Here you go," Rob said, handing her the fallen papers, effectively bringing her back to the reason she was in his office. Ben stood, too. "This way, please."

Zoe followed, but remained acutely aware that Ben was behind her every step of the way. She felt his gaze on her back, hips and legs. Every time she moved she remembered what it was like to have his lips all over her. She shrugged off her shoulder bag and entered a small conference room that resembled a comfortable living room.

"Rob, at the Young Entrepreneurs meeting you gave a lot of tips for working your business. I took a lot of your suggestions to heart, and my business tripled. That could be why I'm having the trouble I am today."

"Not to worry. Hood Investigations doesn't have a near-perfect record for nothing. Some refreshments," Rob suggested.

Zoe helped herself to water. "Near perfect?" she queried, sitting down, crossing her legs. "That's impressive. One got away?" She looked between the two men and a sliver of darkness passed between them that was at once hot and cold and deadly.

"There's always one that we'd like to have done better. But that's it. One," Rob said. Danger and safety commingled then retreated to their respective corners.

"What's going on, Zoe?" Ben asked. "I read the report and wondered why the last three break-ins hadn't been reported to the police."

She put her water on the coaster and pulled out her computer. "I'm planning an expansion worth millions. I've been warned by the mall owner that if my loss numbers, which are theft or shrinkage numbers, don't decrease, I'll lose all the money I've invested. The owner of the mall has stated that his insurance rates increase the more incident reports the police respond to. He will not bear a greater liability because I can't control theft in my store. If I can't resolve this theft issue, he'll drop my bids for future business in his malls, and I'll lose my investment."

"That hardly seems fair," Rob said. "Who is this?"

"Mitch Turner of MT Worldwide Development."

"I've heard of them. I thought they were a reputable

outfit, but this sounds questionable. Let's back up." Ben said. "How much have you invested already?"

"A million and a half dollars. That's for two additional stores. I have two now. Zoe's Diamonds on Peachtree, and Zoe's Diamonds at the Galleria."

Ben nodded. "Do you have any idea who might be breaking into your stores?"

"No."

"You've done background checks on everyone? Staff, workmen, and the like?"

Zoe smoothed a wide curl behind her ear. "Staff only. If we're remodeling, then it's the company's responsibility to do a background check on all their employees and provide the paperwork to me. For me to do it would be cost prohibitive."

"That could be how you're getting robbed."

"Excuse me?" Zoe turned to Ben. "If they're going to be there five days or more, I do a background check."

"That's your criteria?" Ben drummed his fingers on the edge of the table.

"I do a standard criminal background check. A more in-depth check is counterproductive for a retail outfit. At fifty dollars a pop, I can't afford to do a more expensive check on someone who might quit after two days."

"Has that happened?"

"It happens all the time."

Zoe realized he was asking typical questions and reined in her defensive responses. Ben was just doing his job.

"What's the average salary for sales associates?" Ben asked.

"They start at ten an hour and the highest is fifteen plus commission."

The room was quiet for a while and her defenses slid

up again. "These people make a decent hourly wage. With expansion plans, I can't afford to pay more right now, but we're competitive."

"Zoe, you don't have to defend your salaries."

"Thank you, Rob. I want to add that the bad guys seem to be one step ahead of me. A few weeks ago I forgot my purse at work and since I was only twenty minutes away I turned around and went back. In that short amount of time they'd been in and out of the store."

"How'd they get in?"

"I'm not sure, but the front gate was unlocked when I got there. I'm positive I locked it before I left. It's the last thing I do."

"Who has keys?" Ben asked.

"The three opening and closing managers. I do. My father. That's a total of five people."

Ben's look was skeptical. "Your father?"

"That's right. Captain Anthony McKnight of the Fulton County PD. As far as I'm concerned, his gun is as good as any to shoot a bad guy. But he's currently on disability."

"Of course," Rob said. "I know your father. When I was a detective, we worked on a joint task force for a case. I visited him when he was hit by the driver who didn't stop on I285. Quite a heroic officer to put his life before his rookies. I hope he's getting better."

Zoe smiled. "Wow, Rob. I had no idea. Dad has had so many visitors, it's hard to keep up. He's on the mend, thanks for asking. I've got my dad's keys on me. I picked them up last week because I knew I was going to have an appointment with you and I thought you might ask for them." Zoe kept her focus on Rob. "Can you help me?"

"We can. I want to reassure you that you're in the right place. Whoever is doing this is going to be sorry. Ben will be the lead investigator on your case. He's good. In fact, my brother is the best."

"I see." She slid the wild curl that refused to be tamed behind her ear and ignored it when it popped out again. "Is there anyone else?"

Ben laughed and closed Zoe's folder. "You heard the lady, Rob. Is there anyone better than me?"

"That wasn't her question."

"No, it wasn't. This isn't personal, Ben," she told him, knowing she was lying.

"Why would you want second best?" Ben's demand was so gentle she nearly apologized for being foolish.

The probing question was both personal and professional and she couldn't deal with answering him now. Not in front of Rob who didn't need to be dragged through the murk of her failed one-night stand.

Eventually, the memories of their encounter would fade like all memories did.

"I don't want second best. But if we're going to work together, I want a guarantee. Two weeks is what you have to get this mystery solved."

"That's not how we work, Zoe. It's unrealistic to put a time frame on something of this nature," Rob told her in a kind but frank manner. "This has been going on for over four weeks. We may break this case in a week or a month, but we can't work with that time frame until we can do an in-depth assessment."

"Deal." Ben sounded both strong and confident. "But, if at any time your safety is endangered, or we find evidence of something big, we reserve the right to adjust the time frame."

"Ben," his brother warned. "That might be a little unrealistic, but I'll defer to your judgment."

"We'll start with two weeks, and let Zoe decide if she wants to walk away at the end of that time."

Silence gripped the room.

"That's fair," Rob agreed.

"We're talking petty crimes here," Zoe objected. "Probably the work of the smash-and-grab ATM thieves who have graduated to jewelry. I don't want this blown out of proportion, Ben."

"I wouldn't count sixty-five thousand dollars a petty crime. Zoe's Diamonds on Peachtree was hit for a little over ten thousand, and the Galleria store was for fifty-five thousand dollars over the last two months."

Her heart pounded. "I see you did your research."

"In preparation of our meeting, we did some checking and found out that not only was a three-carat pair of earrings, platinum cufflinks and a gold and diamond tennis bracelet stolen from your store, plus—"

"Yes, I know, but—"

"Let me finish. They haven't turned up in any pawn shop, either, so they were stolen for personal use and can be on ice for a long time before someone decides the public has forgotten about them. Other items were stolen from another jewelry store seven miles from the mall.

"A platinum-and-white-diamond tiara worth eighteen thousand dollars. Gold cuff bracelets are worth five, and unset diamonds wholesale for fifteen. You didn't see this in the news because they aren't insured. The owner didn't want people coming around thinking his store was fair game."

The notion sent shivers down Zoe's spine. "That's crazy. Why weren't they locked in a safe?" She didn't realize she'd sat forward until she heard Ben speak in a confidential tone.

"They were. The manager had just left and the silent

alarm was tripped. She went back and was seriously injured. Her arm was broken."

"Oh. Well, hell."

"Yes, let's continue."

"I assume they got away."

"Correct. It was never reported. The tiara wasn't insured and never recovered, I'm afraid."

Cold fear struck Zoe in the chest. "All of my jewelry is insured, except I haven't reported all the break-ins because I don't want my premiums to skyrocket and I don't want to lose my investment. I figured I could take the hit once. But this has happened three times. Hiring this firm is my Hail Mary."

"Then we take no chances. You do what I ask and we work together. Okay?"

"Okay, but you have to understand, I have a business to run and this feels so overwhelming. I want to be able to have fun with my customers, and do shows, and loan out jewelry. That's how Zoe's got its name."

Ben hated bargainers, but he went along with it to appease Zoe and his brother. He'd deal with each incident as it arose. "Fine, but loaning jewelry to celebrities or politicians must be preapproved and only after a background check."

"Okay," she finally agreed.

"Well, it sounds like we'll be working together. Welcome to Hood Investigations. We're going to solve this problem, Zoe." Rob stood, and shook her hand.

"Thank you. I appreciate your time."

"You're welcome. My next appointment will be here in a few moments. I'll leave you in Ben's capable hands."

She looked into her untouched water, her cheeks remembering the capability of Ben's hands. "Of course. Take care, Rob."

The door closed, and Ben set down a fresh cup of water for her and a cup of coffee for himself.

"Oh, no, thank you," she said in a rush. "I brought a flash drive of our day-to-day schedule of operations. I expect you'll want to do an in-store visit, maybe as a customer. You'll be able to see things from your own perspective. Also, posing as a customer, the staff won't know who you are and you can get a feel for them. I trust them implicitly, but that may be the problem. I have to get going. I've got a full day ahead. Here's the drive. The schedule is on there, as well as the staff with photos. Signed confidentiality agreements are also included. I thought that would be helpful. And—" she opened her bag and pulled out the check she'd endorsed last night. "Your fee. I'll see you later, I'm sure."

She got to the door, her hand on the knob. She'd never spoken so fast.

"Zoe, come here."

His voice reached into her and took her places she'd not been since she'd been with him. The resonance offered assurances it didn't have the right to give. He wasn't her man and he wasn't even commanding her, and her body felt like responding. But the yellow caution sign in her brain flashed bright.

Her hand wouldn't obey the command to open the door. "Sit down, Zoe. We need to discuss the ground rules when it comes to you and me."

"What? Why?" She laughed, but heard how grating it sounded and stopped. "There is no you and me."

"While we're working together, this relationship has to remain professional at all times. I can't and won't sleep with you."

She sat down then. "That's a little presumptuous since I didn't ask you the first time. But that's fine. Agreed."

"Good. Since that's out of the way, I'll have to know about all your lovers. You could be a target because of one of them. Or one of them could be using you. Names, addresses and phone numbers. If you'd be more comfortable, you can write it down yourself. But I'll have to check them out. Personally."

Chapter 3

"I have half a mind to take my check and walk out of here."

Zoe's portfolio hit the table and her no-nonsense glare reminded him that she was a successful businesswoman for a reason. He'd more than struck a nerve. He'd plowed into the circuit board. Her eyebrows were raised and she looked as if she was about to ball up her fists and take the first swing.

Ben rolled the pen through his fingers. "I'm not making any judgments." Though he was. He wanted to know all of her business. Why she hadn't called? Why hadn't she returned his calls? If there was someone else keeping her warm at night. Life had an explanation for everything, and he could accept the explanation of being busy, but not another man. Not after their night together.

"Ben, don't lie. You're definitely making judgments. I don't sleep around, and the implication that I can't control myself around you is ludicrous."

"I'm sorry I offended you." The check was still between them on the table. Rob would kill him if Zoe's check didn't clear the bank because he'd allowed a personal matter to interfere with business. "It's just that we have history. A short history, but it's there, so I thought we should talk about it."

"There's nothing between us, Ben. Not that I didn't want it to be, but I need to get my new stores launched and established. And I don't have time for a personal life right now."

Maybe he just had to accept that sex was all it had been to her. Glancing over the fuchsia dress that hugged her curves, he forced his mind back to winning the account he was presently losing. "I just didn't want there to be a problem between us because I didn't call you back."

"Hold on one second. I didn't call *you* back." Her eyes narrowed. "I get the reverse game going on here." She shifted her hands from side to side. "I remember what you said that night at the party. 'I allow the woman to set the pace of the relationship because I don't want her to feel as if she's being rushed into anything. She can call me after the first date,' and I didn't!"

"You're right, I did say that. I'm saying from this moment on, everything between us has to remain strictly business. At some point, I may be trying to save your life and I don't want you second guessing me because of some history—like now."

Ben put the check in the folder and typed on a keyboard installed beneath the table where he sat. "You made the right decision calling us. We're going to find out who's robbing you and we'll put an end to it."

The lights in the room dimmed.

"There are six members of the Hood team. You need to know who they are by sight. There's Rob and me. There is Hugh, my first cousin. He's the camera-and-computer specialist. Zachary is my younger brother and the security expert. Then there is Amelia, known as Mel, and she's part of Hood Trap Team and Alexandria, known as Xan, the head of Hood Trap Team."

Zoe looked at the presentation of the photos and it faded and the lights automatically came on in the room. "Will they all be working on my case?"

"Possibly, but only as needed. Right away, I'm going to have Hugh go in and work on installing our cameras in the stores."

"What does Trap Team do?"

"Whatever is necessary to get the job done. They're specialists at catching liars and cheaters."

Zoe nodded. "I can see how that may be beneficial." After her morning conversation with Faye, Zoe felt the need to be thorough and not leave any ambiguity regarding her position on what happened between them. "I hope you understand, Ben."

"What?" He walked over to the station and pulled off a sheet of paper, read it and handed it to her.

"My reasons for everything."

"I said I did and I do. Here's your receipt. We need to get started. Go back to your store and I'll see you there in about an hour. Don't acknowledge me when I come in. I'd like to see how far I can get away with things. Are the rules regarding employee conduct and store policies on the flash drive, as well?"

"Yes, it's all there." He was all business and that made her want him to slow things down a bit and talk things through. Zoe recognized she couldn't have it both ways.

"Good. We'll see if I can spot anything unusual going on. I may have some of the team with me or I may be alone. Try not to be on the floor if that's not where you'd normally be."

"Okay. Anything else?"

"You'll have to give me a complete schedule of every place you're going to be every second of your day until this is solved. No secrets. No surprises. You and I are going to be tighter than conjoined twins."

"That close?" she asked with a small laugh.

"Like skin and deodorant."

Zoe rubbed her neck. "Do you suspect anyone, Zoe? That could save us a lot of time."

"A former manager, Tori Brunelle. She wanted more money than I was willing to pay, and before she left, things started disappearing. I let her go and changed the locks, but I believe she still has influence over some of the staff. I've even replaced some of them, but you never know how people know one another."

"I'll add her to the list of the current staff to do checks on. Anybody else?"

"Not that I can think of." Zoe shouldered her bag and walked to the door. "Ben, we have to keep this confidential because if my sister gets wind that we had a thing, well, my family gets nosy."

"They won't hear about us from me. You and I will have a code if you're in trouble. I'll be the doctor calling with your test results. You'll tell me it's a bad time to talk. If there's one bad guy, say the baby is kicking a lot today. Two bad guys, the twins. Three, the triplets. Do you understand, Zoe?"

She nodded. "Is all this necessary?"

Ben spread his hands. "You never know what you're going to need to know."

The door opened, and the male receptionist that initially greeted her poked his head inside. "Excuse me, Ben, Ms. McKnight? The police were on the phone for you, but we got disconnected."

"Why?"

"I had your sister first, but she hung up to talk to them. She said your cell phone dialed the store and she could hear your meeting. She was trying to call and tell you that your store just got robbed. When she couldn't reach you, she called the police. Then they called us."

Panicked, Zoe jumped up. "She has to cancel them. There can't be a report."

Zoe pushed the button on her Treo handheld for the store, but nobody answered. She dialed Faye's cell but got no answer. "I've got to stop her. I told her to go home and help my father, but no. She had to help me." She grabbed her portfolio and started for the door.

"I'm going with you." They hurried up front and the receptionist handed Ben his jacket, taking the folder from Ben's hand.

"You can't." Zoe trotted toward the exit. "Nobody is supposed to know about you."

"Are you arguing already?"

"No. I'm not. No." She took a deep breath. "Can you guarantee me that you're going to get these bloodsucking scumbags?" Zoe dug into her purse for her car keys. "Promise, or I'm buying a bigger clip for my .45."

Ben offered his hand to Zoe as they headed out of the building. "I promise. But you go in first and let me make my own entrance. I need to see things from my own perspective."

"I'll see you there."

Chapter 4

Zoe entered the upscale mall at the lower-level south entrance, passing through the food court. The blending of Thai, Chinese and fast food odors usually made her hungry but today roiled her stomach. The casual lunch crowd formed jagged lines. She decided to take the escalator rather than the stairs so that she could quickly assess.

She'd chosen the second-floor corner for her boutique because she'd wanted to be able to say *park at the south entrance, come through the food court, and we're at the top of the escalator.* People would be able to find her easily. The strategy had worked well. Sales had quadrupled since she'd opened three years ago and like she'd told Rob, tripled over the last months.

Zoe's unique designs had brought a renewed sense of excitement to a business that was now saturated with trolley-cart vendors that sold inferior products at lower prices. Today's incident wasn't helping as customers were turned away by two cops who stood outside the doorway.

Bold onlookers still craned to see inside, but there wasn't anything going on. Nobody was in custody and Zoe's heart sank. That would have made her day.

Ireland, one of Zoe's managers, was irritated, gesturing in big sweeping motions as she talked, and when the officer seemed to ask her to settle down, her neck went back, and she gave him a piece of her mind.

As Zoe walked toward the store, she noticed that none of the cases were broken, and while she was thankful, fury burned her. How had they gotten her this time?

Zoe turned, and Ben was behind her. "I thought you were going to stay incognito," she said, startled to see him. The reassurance she felt was hard to hide. She'd reached out and gripped his arm and was about to pull her hand back when he touched her hand in a reassuring way. "I'd planned to, but I changed my mind."

"Why? We had an agreement."

"Hugh's on his way to do the camera work and I want to hear everything you hear, Zoe. I don't want you to have to relay anything to me. I'm going to try to work within your two-week time frame, so let me do my job."

Zoe had a brief flashback to the moment when Ben picked her up in his arms and she had the best orgasm of her life. She'd been weightless and there had been nothing to support her but him. She'd had to put all of her trust in him. "Trust me," he said.

"I'll do my best." She approached the uniformed officers. "This is my store. I'm Zoe McKnight, the owner. I'd like to go in."

"You got ID?"

Irritated, Zoe withstood the visual inspection of herself

and her ID, her patience slipping toward anger that the cop wouldn't let her in until Ireland acknowledged her. The statuesque blonde stalked over. "What the hell do you have her standing here for? She owns the damned place!"

Ben walked in and moved unobtrusively to the side while the cop corralled Zoe and Ireland in the center of the store.

"We were scared," Ireland said, "but I kicked ass and got the jewelry back."

Zoe shook her off. "You did what?"

"I chased down the tall guy and got the jewelry back. Initially, there were three of them. The tall guy asked me to model the tiara, plus see some other pieces. No sooner had I unlocked the case and put it on than we were flooded with twenty men, all dressed alike. They were loud, crowding and rushing me and everyone else."

"You chased who? And where did you chase them?" the police officer asked.

Ireland looked at the three of them. "The tall man I told you about," she said to the cop, "I chased him down the escalator to the outside parking lot. I nailed him with my shoe. Got him in the back of the head."

"We'll need that," the cop told her, glancing at her feet.

"You think I'd be wearing it if it were evidence? These are my back-up shoes," she said of the sparkly black kitten heels. She pulled out a clear plastic bag with the other pair of two-inch heels. He took the bag as evidence.

"These are the shoes I had on when I ran him down. I caught up to him and was screaming my head off. He may have seen all these football-player types heading toward the mall entrance and thought he didn't want to explain to them why he was dragging a woman around. I wouldn't let go and he dragged me for a few seconds." She showed them her leg that was still flaky with Georgia clay.

The cop closed his notebook. "I've got this already. If there's nothing else, I'll be leaving."

Ireland's blond hair swung from side to side. "There's nothing more."

"Thank you. When can I get a copy?" Zoe asked.

"Twenty-four hours," the cop said, and walked out the store. Zoe pulled the gate back down and returned to Ireland and Ben. There were still interested onlookers outside, but she hadn't decided whether she was going to reopen today or not. She needed to hear what happened and then talk to Ben.

"Zoe, I know your policy on chasing crooks, but he stole the necklace from the O'Sullivan collection, and I wasn't going to lose one of those pieces."

"You crazy girl," Zoe admonished. "Are you okay? Do you need to go to the hospital?"

"For what? Tussling with a man?" She looked Zoe straight in the eye. "I had worse fights when I was a kid."

"Those pieces are insured, as is everything in this store," Zoe told her, shaking her head. Her heart was pounding. "Ireland, I should suspend you. You could have been killed. What if they'd had guns? How would I have explained that to your family?"

"Mr. O'Sullivan made those pieces for his wife and he adds a piece to his collection every year. I wasn't going to lose them to some two-bit hustler. I didn't feel like he was a killer. I know it sounds silly. I just didn't feel in imminent danger."

Ben touched Zoe's arm. "I think she's gotten your point." He extended his hand and they shook. "Ben Hood, I work with Zoe. I'd like to know if you remember anything more about the man who asked to see the tiara?"

"Remember the remake of the movie *The Thomas Crown Affair* with Pierce Brosnan? Remember the part with the bowler hats? These guys were all dressed in jeans, white T-shirts, and sneakers. When they left, each put on a Yankees baseball cap. Kind of like they're yanking our chain. When they walked in here, I got a weird feeling."

"Can you put it into words?" Zoe asked.

"There was one guy who asked a lot of questions about the tiara. How many diamonds, the weight, etcetera. He wanted to know if he could have his jeweler do his own tests to authenticate the stones."

"You said no?" Ben asked.

Ireland folded her arms over her chest. "That's right. He told me his name was Rodrigo Martinez and I told him it was an insult to bring his expert into our store without talking to you first. He flirted, but I told him if he didn't like my answer he could take it up with you."

"Where was Faye?" Zoe noticed the two mall security guards head down the mall.

"We were supposed to be working this same side of jewelry cases, while Debrena had the left side and Charletta had the right. But there were so many men in the store, I didn't notice that Faye was gone until it was too late."

"Faye was gone where?" Zoe demanded. She'd expressly told Faye to help Ireland. It was as if the criminals had used her to facilitate their robbery.

Ireland's cheeks turned pink with anger. "Faye had stepped outside the store and was leaning on the front window like a high-school sophomore talking to one of the men. I called her a couple times and even signaled Debrena to get her, but she never looked up."

"Ireland, are you telling me Faye couldn't hear you? There's only fifteen feet of space between here and the door."

"That's right. The noise level was so loud, I could hardly hear myself think. I walked over to Faye's station, saw the open case and the O'Sullivan jewels missing and I thought

I was going to be sick to my stomach. I closed the case and secured the tiara."

"Okay, Ireland. Were you able to provide the officers with a detailed description of the man?"

She nodded.

"Why do you really think Faye stepped outside?" Ben asked Ireland.

"Faye is selfish, and she's jealous of Zoe. She's trying to sabotage her sister's success. Zoe, perhaps you don't see it, but that's the truth."

Hearing the words she'd thought all her life was worse than suspecting them. But she'd always tried to make nice with Faye for the sake of their family. Her mother insisted they put up a front of unity to the world and handle their differences behind closed doors. Only those uncomfortable issues had never been resolved.

"Did she leave the case open intentionally?" Zoe barely managed to get the words out.

"I don't believe in coincidences," Ireland said definitively. "She's been in back the whole time and hasn't come out to see how things are going or to express her sorrow. Yet Debrena's stuck her head out that door fifteen times. You're Faye's sister and this is your store. With that kind of sister, you don't need enemies."

"Where's the tiara now?" Ben asked.

Ireland drew back, her expression closed for the first time.

"Please, Ireland, you can trust Ben. *I* trust him." Zoe's heart skipped a beat at the true statement. "I want to know, too. Where is it?"

"In the floor."

Zoe didn't move. Nor did Ireland.

Ben glanced between them. "Ladies, I can't help you if you don't tell me everything."

Zoe understood the jeopardy of full disclosure. She now had to put her words into practice.

"Ben, when I first designed my store, I thought it would be good to have an extra measure of safety. I designed a floor safe. The problem is that you have to be at the right position behind the counter to drop merchandise into it, and it isn't cost effective. I only built one. In this store."

"Zoe," Ireland cut in, "I promise it was the right time. The tiara is worth forty thousand dollars. He didn't want to turn over his driver's license, though, as collateral. That's why he couldn't touch it."

Ben nodded. "Smart decision."

"Where was everyone?" Zoe asked.

"At their stations. Mr. Martinez was so intent on the tiara, I couldn't not serve him. I just found it odd that a discerning man like him wasn't disturbed by the noise level and manner of the other men. Unless he wasn't that discerning."

"That's a good observation. What else?" Ben asked.

"He asked pointed questions. The noise level increased and he leaned close to me, frustrated that I wouldn't allow him free access to the tiara. He muttered, so I leaned in. When I straightened, no more than ten seconds later, Faye was outside and the store was full of twenty men dressed alike.

"I called to Faye, signaled Debrena, but she couldn't get Faye's attention. I was still wearing the tiara, but he reached for it and actually got hold if it. I saw that Faye's case was open and the jewels gone. I yanked the tiara from his grasp and activated the safe and the alarm."

"What did Martinez do?" Ben asked.

"He protested. The men in the store got louder. I saw the man who had the O'Sullivan jewels. Suddenly, all the men left going in different directions. I took off after the man with the jewelry."

"Show me the safe and where you were standing," Ben said.

Ireland took him to the floor safe. Both she and Zoe entered their security codes and the doors opened. The tiara sat on its head in three feet of velvet. Zoe donned gloves to lift it out. She examined it. "It's perfect. No harm done."

Ireland's sigh was audible.

"Why did it take both of you to get it out?"

"It's designed as a last effort to save whatever is in your hands or the most valuable merchandise in the store. I didn't want a criminal to be able to bring me back to the store and think they could take everything. If Ireland needed to open it herself, she could activate the doors after twenty-four hours."

"Were you involved with the robbery?" Ben asked Ireland.

"Me?" she exclaimed. "No! Zoe knows I'm devoted to this store and I'd never do anything to hurt her. I wouldn't steal from her."

"In light of the circumstances, you did the right thing. Thank you for protecting the store, Ireland. But everything here can be replaced. Please don't put your life in danger again," Zoe said.

Ben's warning look said he wanted to handle the interrogation, but Zoe had to weigh in. Everything in her said Ireland was telling the truth.

"We need better security, Zoe, that's obvious. Nobody else is getting hit. I talk to the other managers on a daily basis."

"I know. That's why Ben is here. Big changes are in the works."

"Are we going to open today?" Ireland wanted to know.

"Yes," Ben said. "I've got some guys coming over to refit this store with different sensors for the cases. I'd like you to be here as an advisor, Ireland. Can you stand by? You'd be compensated, of course."

A grateful expression crossed her face. "I appreciate that. As long as you find out who's ruining my paycheck, I won't chase bad guys anymore."

"You've got my word on that. I'm trying to keep a low profile," Ben told her.

"Fine with me. I just work here. But you will want to talk to Faye separately from Charletta and Debrena. She's got issues with Zoe and you don't want the other girls hearing. If you choose to keep her on, I don't want her working my shift ever again," she said, and walked through the stockroom door.

Ben held Zoe's arm, stopping her. "I don't believe Ireland's involved, but if what she said is true, this is a personal attack against you."

"I feel the same way. Do you think my sister's involved?" The words hurt worse coming out than when she'd just thought them.

"It sounds like it. Can you deal with having your sister questioned and possibly arrested?"

Chapter 5

The other ladies had been questioned and released and Zoe stood facing her sister in the stockroom.

"Why would I want to sabotage Zoe's business? For your information, I believe she's wasting her money hiring you, and if I had any say, you'd be fired."

Faye hurled the words at Ben. To him, she sounded like a woman who had something to hide.

Watching Faye closely, Ben figured that Zoe had been the reasonable child and Faye the drama queen. They'd been there three hours and the other staff members were gone, their statements supporting Ireland's.

"You're being passive-aggressive again." Faye bit into her sister like a barracuda. "Why don't you just come out and call me a thief?"

"Are you?" He didn't care for Faye the way Zoe did. If she was behind the thefts, this would be the fastest ten thousand dollars Hood I.N.V. had ever earned, and the shortest opportunity he'd ever get at a second chance.

"I'd be stealing from myself if I did. I gave you five thousand dollars to start this business."

"You loaned me the money, and I paid you back thirty days after I opened the doors, Faye."

"So you're the big-shot owner, now. I knew this would go to your head," Faye retorted.

"I didn't say that, Faye. We just got robbed. Someone could have been seriously hurt."

"Including me. Nobody asked if I was all right."

Her false indignation was laughable. "Do you need a ride to the hospital?" Ben offered to entertain her nonsense for a moment. "It's only five minutes away. In fact, if it's critical we don't even have to wait for an ambulance, I can drive you there myself."

"I said I *could have* been hurt. All you're worried about is your precious jewelry." She'd directed the last comment to Zoe, shifting away from Ben's scrutiny. Zoe started to speak, but Ben held up his hand. "Where do you work, Faye?"

"First Bank of Greenville in South Carolina. Why?"

"How long have you been there?"

"Twelve years."

"Vice president?" Ben asked.

"Assistant vice president," she sniffed, her chin elevated.

"Ever heard of Rodrigo Martinez?"

"No."

"Not in all your years with the bank? Wow, I wish I had your memory."

"I can't recall meeting anyone with that name. I may have. Those are two common names. I mean, I don't know." She backpedaled, looking as unsure as she sounded.

"That's odd." Ben knew he had her.

"What's so odd about me not knowing every Martinez in the south?" She tried to laugh but couldn't pull it off so she folded her hands, wiped them together and re-folded them.

"I bet once I complete my investigation Rodrigo Martinez will be from Greenville, South Carolina, just like you. I'll bet when I pull the video on this incident, his expression will probably show that he's surprised to see you when he walked in the store. Wasn't he?"

"No. I mean, I might have said hello. I greeted everyone. We want people to feel at home at Zoe's."

"Oh, please," Zoe groaned.

"I've worked in this store before, and Zoe can *Oh, please* if she wants to, but I stayed today as a favor to her."

"That's right, Ben." Zoe rose from her chair and Ben and Faye watched her. "Faye didn't want to be here. You wanted to come with me, but I told you no, twice. I insisted you stay here and help Ireland."

Ben kept his focus on Faye. "You didn't want to be anywhere close to the robbery you planned. So when the crowd got thick, you slipped outside. Nobody could connect you to the theft. You were here, but you weren't."

"I didn't steal anything!"

"You left the case open, didn't you?" Ben felt her confession coming.

"No."

"You sure? The video will show you leaving the doors open, looking left then right, sliding them open a little more and then slipping out the door. Your friend preoccupied Ireland so that one of the look-alikes could stick his arm in and grab what he wanted. All the time, Ireland is calling you. You heard her, didn't you? How do you think a judge will interpret your role in this little heist?"

"I didn't do anything. I was outside," she said desperately. "A man was interested in me."

"What was his name?"

"Uh. Um…Ricky."

"Martin?" Ben offered.

"What?" Faye blinked rapidly. "Yes. No! I don't know his last name."

"That's the first thing a woman finds out about a man, right, Zoe? His name? Where he works? What's his phone number, Faye? His e-mail? Let's call him now and set up your first date. Who is he, Faye?"

"I don't have to answer you."

"Oh, my God. You really stole from me!" Zoe screamed at her sister.

Tears ran from Faye's eyes. "Are you going to let this happen? I'm your blood."

"And that gives you the right?" Zoe snapped.

"It's just jewelry. I'm your sister! Family is supposed to mean more to you than…stuff."

"Why'd you do it?" Zoe asked.

"The divorce is costing me everything. You wouldn't miss the money from a few necklaces—you have insurance—but this could help me get back on my feet. All you had to do was file a claim and they would have paid you back."

Ben had seen selfishness before, but never like this and never so blatantly between sisters.

"You've always been selfish," Zoe told her. "Jealous. You're so lazy. That's why you wanted to go with me today. All you had to do was ask to borrow the money and I'd have loaned it to you."

Faye slapped the desk. "*Borrow?* I'm assistant vice president of the Greenville Bank. I live in a three hundred fifty thousand dollar house, and I eat tuna out of a can and sleep on an air mattress! I've had to sell everything. I'm not borrowing anything from you, do you hear me? This is the least you can do with your high-and-mighty self. I don't need anybody's help. Fine. Help me, then. Let me walk out of here."

Ben wondered what Zoe was going to do. Faye was clearly trying to take advantage of Zoe who seemed to be intently studying her folded hands.

"Faye, it's too bad your life is a mess, but you don't get to decide you're going to fix it at my expense. Ben, I never thought I'd be saying this, but, call the police in here and have them arrest my sister."

Chapter 6

At his desk late, Ben finished the e-mail report he'd been working on and shut off his computer. He looked down at his running shoes and they reminded him of a sad dog waiting by his chair, wanting to go outside and play.

But his drive to do anything was gone. He needed a change of scenery. Maybe a trip to Florida would do the trick. There was nothing like palm trees and bikinis to change a man's perspective.

Yet he still didn't move a muscle. It was Zoe. He missed being with her and working her case. Granted, he'd closed it a week ago, but he still missed the thought of being with her everyday. Ben pushed himself up, grabbed his keys and called his brother.

"Rob, what you up to?"

"Getting ready to go hiking, why?"

"Just wondering. Bored, really." Ben pushed his sneakers around with his foot.

"You closed the Zoe Diamonds case, I see."

"Open and shut."

"Why not call her? Ask her out?" Rob asked casually.

"I don't think she's interested in me that way. I gave her a lot of opportunities. She didn't bite." She hadn't responded to the necklace and he'd sent that days ago. He'd thought for sure he'd have heard from Zoe by now.

"Bite her," his brother said. "You need to date. It's not a conflict of interest since we're not working with her anymore. Call her and see what she's up to."

"I've been down that road before. She wouldn't even tell me why she stopped dating me before."

"Ben, you act like you're scared of her."

Ben paced his foyer. Was he? Hell no! Zoe didn't scare him. He just didn't want to get knocked down again by her. "I like Zoe. A lot."

"Then why not pursue her?"

"She wouldn't take my calls before the case. What would make her take them now?"

"You're the hero." Rob sounded so confident Ben almost believed him. "You saved her business, recovered her jewels. You're the man."

Ben chuckled. "I think I'll head to Florida this weekend. See what's happening down there."

"You suck at dating, man. You got to keep getting on that horse. Zoe's gorgeous and probably worth going after," Rob told him. "Well, if not Zoe, I told you about Laney, right? She's the friend of mine who does all these crazy trips around the world in the name of peace and philanthropy, and comes back with amazing stories. She's in town tonight, but I have plans. Why don't you two hang out? I can give her your address and she can stop by. She wanted to come by here."

"No. She sounds like she might have a screw loose if she's hanging with you."

"Shut up," Rob told him, laughing. "I have a Young Entrepreneurs meeting tonight or I'd entertain her and a couple friends from the YE meeting. She's really nice. Please, Ben?"

The clock struck seven and he shrugged. "Why not? I don't have anything else to do."

Seven days had passed since Zoe had seen Faye behind bars, and seven long nights had passed since she'd seen Ben. Zoe finished inventory alone in Zoe's Diamonds at the Galleria, proud that every single piece of jewelry had been accounted for. She locked the last case and sat down at her desk in the back of the store.

Ben had really impressed her. He hadn't needed two weeks. He hadn't needed two hours. He'd gotten to the bottom of the thefts in thirty minutes, pressuring Ireland, who'd been honest and innocent, and Faye, who'd been dishonest and guilty. It had been the best ten thousand dollars she'd ever spent. She hadn't lost a piece of jewelry, including the diamond solitaires her sister had been wearing when booked into jail. Ben had even recovered those, too. Faye hadn't lasted more than twenty-four hours before she'd given up Martinez as her accomplice. They'd planned to sell the jewels and split the proceeds. Martinez had been arrested and the case closed to Ben's satisfaction.

All told, he'd saved Zoe's Diamonds nearly sixty-five thousand dollars. She'd been trying to think of a way to thank him, but hadn't been able to come up with one that didn't involve belly button shots of liquor and explosive sex. That's where things would end up, she knew, because she hadn't been able to get him off her mind. What had started out as a post-divorce distraction had turned into something much more.

In her store, looking above her head, she saw the mail hadn't been opened for the day and she pulled out some envelopes and a small package. Hood Investigations was on the label. Zoe opened it, her heart pounding, and pulled out the note. "I found these and I remembered our night together. I'm not returning them. I'm sharing them. Round two to be determined…Ben."

Zoe looked inside the envelope and pulled out a four-by-four inch box. Lifting the lid, she gasped. Inside was the necklace of Tahitian pearls. Inside the lid were earrings to match.

He'd paid for them. Ten thousand dollars. Covering her mouth, she shook her head and sighed. Ben Hood was definitely all man. She would follow her instincts that had been telling her to call him, and she would when she got into her car. She'd experienced his job and it was nothing like her father's job as a police officer. She'd been wrong to judge him so harshly without all the facts. And now that business wasn't between them, naked sweaty skin would be.

Ben did that to her. He made her good, logical, professional sense fly out the window, and turned her into the equivalent of a wanton. She sighed and chewed a stick of sugarless gum.

The past week had been hard not having anyone to talk to. Her parents were split over her having Faye arrested. Her mother believed prayer could heal anything and she should have let Faye go. Her father loved his oldest child, but he was also a cop at heart. He believed a few nights in jail would cure anybody. Zoe and her father were close because they'd shared similar thoughts for years. Faye had problems and she needed help, but robbing Zoe wasn't the way to get over them.

She hadn't agreed with her parents bailing Faye out of jail because she knew they didn't have the money, but that had been their choice. What Zoe hated most was that Faye was now living at their house as a condition of her bail, and things were tense. Zoe missed her evening chats with her parents. She missed sharing her expansion plans with them, and the closeness they'd established over the years since Faye had left Georgia.

Standing up, Zoe stretched her arms over her head, slowly jutting her hip left then right, waiting for her muscles to loosen. Feeling the relief, she breathed deeply and started gathering her things. She was no longer the tomboy who thought she could fly from the fifty-yard line to the goal post.

She stacked everything she needed by the door. This office was functional, but nothing like her plush, comfortable space at home. She'd had the home office decorated last year in reds and browns, with splashes of gold. It was the most joyful place to work in the world.

Smiling, she finished packing her Louis Vuitton duffel bag and made sure the safe was set and locked. She'd set and locked it an hour ago, but being a little obsessive-compulsive wasn't a bad thing given all she'd been through. Tucking her car keys in the waist of her pants, she gathered her duffel and shopping bags into her hands, set the alarm, stepped outside the back door into the service hallway and locked the door to Zoe's.

The first blow grazed the corner of her neck, and her jaw hit the door.

She dropped the bags as she struck back, going for his testicles. He deflected, and seemed surprised by the upper-cut to his jaw. He had no way of knowing about her green belt in Karate.

He kept coming, stunning her with a few blows to her

stomach and face, but she wouldn't be beat, not by him, not by anyone.

"Bitch, you were supposed to be gone!"

She'd learned to never talk trash. She needed all the air in her lungs to fight. But she tried to memorize the tone and inflection of his voice, and every physical feature about him.

He was coming in to finish her off and she felt desperation filling in the blank spaces. He came in fast and she used her elbows, catching his nose, surprising him, and he fell back, holding the displaced flesh, and she dove to the ground for her purse and her .22.

Before she could pull the gun free, he was gone.

Chapter 7

The doorbell interrupted a date that could have ended with Ben walking off into the night and never returning. He'd already heard—in appalling detail—about genital mutilation in some parts of Africa, then had the benefit of watching the insemination process of purebred horses in Oregon. He was to the point where he could comfortably say he could potentially never date again, and not feel a moment of regret.

Laney Sharply-Stanhope, with her blond dreads, wasn't like any holistic healer he'd ever met before. She was a nut, and Ben didn't know what he'd done to his brother to deserve this, but Rob would hear about it tomorrow.

Ben tripped up the step leading to the wide foyer to answer the persistent ringing. "It's getting late, Laney, and I've got an early day tomorrow," he said over his shoulder.

"It's only nine-fifteen." She laughed, staying in the den.

"Your brother warned me about you. Invite your company to join us. The more the merrier. I've got a USB flash on my keychain and you've got your laptop. We can look at photos of my trip to Africa." He almost laughed aloud at the murderous plot that ran through his head.

Peering through the peephole, he saw Zoe's curls and knew it was trouble. She hadn't been to his house since their night together, and she wouldn't have come if she didn't need something.

Pulling the wide door open, he reached for her and saw the side of her face in the moonlight. "What the hell happened?"

Her nose was bleeding and she had a gun in her left hand. "I was attacked."

Ben peeled the gun from her fingers and pocketed it. Pulling her into his arms, he helped her inside, checking the perimeter before closing the door. "It's going to be all right. Did you shoot him?"

She shook her head. "I wanted to so bad and the asshole ran." The tissues she held were ineffective.

"That's okay. You left him for me."

He tried to get a good look at her but she braced and he held her longer. She nodded against his shoulder as if she were trying to come to some agreement within herself to stay calm.

"You're dressed up. Are you on a date?" she said.

She was calm and that was a testament to her strength. "Yes. Not really."

"Oh, hell. Sorry to interrupt." She caught her breath. "I need you, Ben. I want Hood to do what Hood does and kill the son-of—"

He put his finger to her lips and winced. They were getting fatter by the second. "I get your drift. Don't worry about my date. You did me a favor."

"That bastard hit me in my face." Anguish made her features crumble and his heart nearly broke. She was in shock, her eyes wide and glassy. He pulled his cell from his belt and dialed his brother. "Rob, get to my house now. Zoe's been assaulted."

"Where is he?" she asked.

"Rob lives four houses down the street. But he's at a meeting. He'll be here soon." He pulled her purse off her shoulder, dropping it onto the chair. "Whoever did this is going to get his ass beat Hood style."

A sob tore from her and she wrapped her arms around his waist. "Tonight I wish I were a Hood. I'd have gotten him."

He knew she didn't realize what she'd said with her arm around him, the other holding her nose closed. But her words reached inside and swayed him like a political swing vote.

"Ben, is everything all right?" He heard Laney call from the den.

Just that quickly he'd forgotten about his date. "Laney, something's come up. I'm sorry, but I really do have to cut our evening short."

"Okeydokey," she said, as Ben guided Zoe to the bathroom. "I'll see myself out."

Two big tears streaked down Zoe's cheeks and the hand around his waist tightened in thanks. "I think my tooth is loose." She inhaled deeply, holding her head back in an effort to stop crying. She tried to look in the mirror, but Ben nudged her.

"Would you sit down, please? I'm in charge in this bathroom, Ms. McKnight."

Anger rocked him. Whoever did this to her would pay. "This happened at work?"

Sitting her on the commode, he wet large black washcloths and began to dab gently at her face. She raised her arm and winced, scaring him.

"Zoe, I'm not a doctor. We're going to the hospital. I insist."

"I just want to stay here." Her voice quivered and tears ran from the corners of her eyes. "I don't like being scared, and I was terrified he was going to kill me." A sob broke from her. "I took karate so no one would hurt me, and he beat me up."

"He didn't, baby. You got away."

She looked up at him, her face swelling, tearing him apart. "He only got away after I went for my gun. I was too scared. I should have shot him. I should have taken him down. Why is this happening to me?" she cried.

Ben didn't know what to do. He didn't have any answers. He'd thought the problem was solved and he was wrong. This was his fault. He tried not to dissect the case right now, but he couldn't help himself. What had he missed? He'd have to start over from the beginning, from the second he received her e-mail file from Rob, to the police questioning of Ireland, to the booking of Zoe's sister into jail. He'd underestimated the perpetrators, thinking Faye had been the only one. So that left the only other possibility. Someone else was after Zoe's business.

He'd made a critical error and not gone into enough depth and as a result, Zoe had been vulnerable and was now seriously hurt.

Ben picked her up and put her on his lap. He held her in his arms and comforted her. "Zoe, the best fighters don't always knock their opponents to the ground."

Her body shook. "He was hitting my torso and a few to my face and I was frozen. All I could do was block. I dropped my bags and I could have used them to protect my body. I forgot everything I learned," she cried. "I finally came up with my elbows and struck him in the nose."

Ben heard his brothers in the hallway talking.

"What was that?" Her head popped up and her hands closed into fists. Ben brought her closer.

"Rob is out there, and probably my brother Zach." Ben rubbed her back to soothe her.

Rob took that moment to knock on the door. He came in and swore under his breath. He lightly touched Zoe's shoulder. "Zoe, I'm so sorry. Believe me when I say we're going to find out who did this and make them regret ever touching you."

"Thank you, Rob. I don't think I need the hospital, but Ben is insisting."

"You do." Rob helped her stand and Ben took her hand. She was limping and in the bright bathroom light every bruise was apparent on her smooth skin.

"My chest hurts. He had something on his hand."

"Where?" Ben asked.

Zoe pointed right beneath her collarbone and he peeled down the neck line of her top. Both Ben and Rob examined the bruise. "Some kind of ring mark maybe," Rob guessed.

Ben nodded. "I'll see if they can get a picture of it. Come on. Let's get there before any more time gets away. Zoe, Rob and Zach will put a plan together on what's going to happen from here on."

"Let me know what they say. Do you need anything?" Rob asked, as he led them out the bathroom.

"Ice," Ben said.

"I'll get it," his brother Zachary said, who'd been standing in the hallway the whole time. He was the joker of the family, but in serious times, Zach was a force to be reckoned with. Wider and bigger than both Ben and Rob, Zach could get mean quick.

Zoe held her left arm close to her ribcage. "I'm a little bruised, but nothing is broken." She was shaking. "I just want to go home."

Ben and his brother exchanged glances, but didn't say anything else. "Check in later," Rob told him. "We're going by the Peachtree Diamonds' location just to check things out."

"Rob?" Zoe said, wiping her tears.

"Yes?" They huddled close to her, forming a protective circle. She brought her hand up to his arm and he covered it with his.

"He said, 'Bitch, you were supposed to be gone.' I stayed behind to finish inventory and I let the others go home. I just wanted to get it finished tonight. I was happy that all the jewelry was accounted for. I opened some mail, and then gathered my things to leave."

"What time were you supposed to be gone?"

"Nine o'clock. The mall closes at nine."

She turned into Ben's chest and cried. Rob patted her back. "Please don't worry, Zoe. We're going to take care of this. You two go ahead."

Ben took the wrapped ice pack Zach offered. When Ben moved Zoe's hair, they winced at the bruise on her neck. "Zach, get over there and get the video. I never had the chance to have Hugh outfit the place with cameras, but I noticed there are some cameras in the mall near the store."

"Who is Hugh again?" Zoe asked.

"He's our cousin and our computer expert," Ben explained.

"I was in the service hallway," Zoe explained as they walked out the front door, and he helped her into the Range Rover. "There's only one camera out there."

Rob buckled her in the seat and put the ice pack on her ribs.

Ben ran around his truck and slid in. "Zachary, get that video. I want to see it when I get back."

"I'll have it and the guard, too, if necessary." Zach and Rob watched them pull off, but Ben drove away knowing Zach meant business.

The emergency waiting room was half-full when Ben escorted Zoe inside. They walked up to the desk and he pulled out a pen and handed it to her.

"Just sign in and the doctor will be with you in about a half an hour. This shouldn't take more than two hours, max."

Zoe looked at him. "You seem to know the routine."

"I've been here a time or two." He caressed her cheek with his thumb. "I'm so sorry."

Zoe started the paperwork and then stopped.

"What's the matter?" he asked.

"I feel like I got the mess kicked out of me. But I don't feel bad enough to be here."

Ben took the clipboard and leaned back in the chair. "You need to be here. Sit back."

Zoe hated the way people in the room were looking at her. Hated that they were judging her and Ben. She wanted to get in her bed and have a good cry. She wanted this to be a bad dream, not some living nightmare. She slowly pushed back in her chair and turned her face into Ben's shoulder.

"What, Zoe?"

"I just don't want to be here. I want to cry, that's all."

"I know you do. Let's find out that you're okay, then you can cry as much as you want for one night. Then we're kicking ass starting tomorrow, okay?"

A giggle shook her chest and she put her head on his shoulder. "I like you, Ben. I like the way you think."

He rubbed her knee. "Girl, you're making me blush. Now about this form… How much do you weigh?"

"You're not funny." Zoe took the clipboard and completed the questions herself.

An hour later the doctor completed her exam and allowed her to get dressed.

"Will you call Mr. Hood inside please? He needs to hear this." Zoe stretched her sore muscles.

"You're sure you want him in here?" The doctor was a bespectacled Asian man with pleasant features and bright eyes, despite the early-morning hour.

Zoe nodded. "Ben didn't do this to me. I was attacked at my job by someone I don't know. Mr. Hood brought me to the hospital. He's my friend." Zoe didn't want to explain further. It was three in the morning. She just wanted to climb between her sheets and forget this night ever happened.

The doctor allowed Ben into the room.

As soon as he walked in, he touched her back and she felt more at ease. "Ms. McKnight, you have two bruised ribs, a minor concussion and some abrasions. The bruises will fade and the ribs will be sore for a week or so. I'd say that green belt saved you. I'm most concerned about the ribs."

"Not the concussion?" Ben asked.

The doctor shook his head pointing to the X-ray. "This is close to being a hairline fracture. You're going to be sore tomorrow, but take the medication and rest. The concussion is minor. You'll have a headache."

Ben was gentle with her as he caressed her arm. "Is there anything else she's going to need to do to get better?"

"The concussion is going to require some rest. No work for three to five days and ibuprofen for the pain. I'd have her follow up with her regular doctor in three days, but until then, stay away from work and no sparring or fighting."

"Can I go home?" Zoe asked.

"Is there anyone there to help you for a couple days?" the doctor asked.

Zoe shook her head. "Just me," she said.

"I'd enlist the help of your bodyguard here, a family member or friend." His smile was sympathetic. "You don't need to be admitted, but you can't be alone with a concussion."

"You can stay at my house," Ben offered.

"No, Ben. I'll go to my parents.'" Weariness washed over her as soon as she finished the statement. Faye was staying with her parents, and Zoe knew they couldn't co-exist under the same roof given the circumstances. "I can go to a hotel. They can wake me up every few hours."

Ben shook his head as she rattled off other possibilities. "Or you can stay with me."

"Fine, Ben. I'll stay with you." She thought about it and sighed, realizing it was the best option.

"Thank you."

A half hour later, they were on their way home, the wet street creating halos under the lamplights.

"Are you hungry?" Ben asked.

"No, thank you."

"You should eat before taking that medicine."

She swallowed two pills and drank from the eight-ounce bottle of water they'd given her at the hospital pharmacy, their last stop before leaving. "I'm not hungry. Ben, thanks again—"

"Let me stop you right there. I'm not doing you a favor. I feel terrible that you're hurt, and until you're better and your case resolved, I'm not going to leave your side."

Zoe closed her eyes, and felt his voice inside her body and was comforted by it. The masculine tone seemed to bind to her and she felt safe again. His hands were warm when he touched hers, when he wrapped his arms around her, and when he carried her into the house and to the bedroom. Her eyes fluttered open when he laid her on the bed. "I thought I was dreaming that you carried me."

"No dream." He smiled as he kneeled in front of her and carefully loosened the tie waistband of her pants.

Her body felt heavy and she realized slowly that the medicine had begun to take effect. Her muscles didn't hurt so much anymore. She'd been given a T-shirt at the hospital, her top having been stained with blood. "I want to take this T-shirt off. It's scratching me."

"Let me get you another one." Ben got up and went into the bathroom. "This one is really big, but it should do until we can get some of your things."

Zoe nodded. "I'll have to buy something. I don't wear pajamas. They get twisted in the sheets."

Ben gathered the bottom of the T-shirt and helped her take it off, sliding the other on with less difficulty. It swam around her thighs, but Zoe didn't care. Ben started on her belt again. "I can undo my pants," she said quietly, and sat up.

"Are you sure?" He looked at her and she wanted to bring his head to her chest and hold him there. But she couldn't. Not after her dismissive thoughts of him and the fact that she'd disrespected him by not calling. *The necklace.* She still hadn't mentioned it. She'd have to tell him she'd received it another time.

Zoe made several attempts to undo her pants, but her hair kept getting in the way, and her hands weren't working right anymore. "I give up," she said, looking into his eyes, her shoulders feeling like they were weighed down by bags of sand.

"Let me help you."

"Thank you, Ben."

"Zoe, stop thanking me. I haven't done anything yet."

She gazed at him and felt the tears coming. "You opened the door tonight and that means a lot to me."

"Of course I did, sweetheart. Anytime you need me, I'm here."

"Don't be nice to me after I didn't call you back," she said, wiping her tears. She held his shoulders and stood up, letting the pants slide down her legs. Sitting on the bed, she felt the cloak of sadness cover her.

"At the time, you reminded me of everything I hated when I was a kid. I was always afraid that my father wasn't going to come home. When I heard you talk about a warrant and picking someone up, I freaked out and ran."

Ben chuckled. "Zoe, we can talk about this later."

"No. I should have called if I said I was going to."

"Okay. Did you want to?"

She nodded. "Many times." The tears flowed and she let them come, finally giving in to the sadness of what had been happening to her.

"Is that the only reason you called Hood Investigations?"

"No, Rob was one reason, but…you were the second."

Ben urged her to lie down. "I'm always second to that bum," he joked. "Just because he was born four minutes earlier, that makes him better?"

Rain pounded the roof of the house and made the tree leaves sound like they were laughing.

"Baby, don't cry."

"I feel terrible. Why would someone want to hurt me? I don't have any enemies. I don't do bad things. I'm a good person."

"I know you are."

She snuffled and he went to the bathroom and got some

tissues for her face. Wiping her eyes, he kissed her forehead. "Are you finished?"

It was Zoe's turn to chuckle. "I haven't even started."

Ben laughed. "Come on, Zoe. Nobody is going to hurt you anymore," he cajoled. "I already made you some promises. What did I tell you?"

"You'd kick their asses?"

He nodded. "What else?"

"You'd make them sorry to know me and…I forgot."

"You forgot," he teased, dabbing her tears, pretending indignation.

"I have a concussion," she said, just above a whisper. "You have to be nice to me."

"Aww, baby. I'm nice to you. I said I was never leaving your side."

"I'm so thankful. I wanted to stop at the police station, but I didn't put in a report because I was scared I'd lose my investment. I can lose a few pieces of jewelry if I stay focused on the big picture. But I can't lose 1.5 million dollars."

Tears streamed from her eyes and he wiped them. "You're going to achieve your dreams. Stop thinking so much and rest."

"I have to say this while it's on my mind, Ben."

"What is it, baby?" He tucked her in and smoothed back the mass of natural curls.

"Something inside of me had to see you again. It wasn't just physical. It was the same thing that brought me to your door tonight. It's you, Ben. The man that you are. I trust you. I like you." Zoe closed her eyes, her fingers laced with his.

"That means a lot to me." He smoothed her hair again and she pushed it back.

His gaze caressed her and she wished she knew what he was thinking. He was so quiet, so gentle with her, her resistance to him faded the minute he'd opened the door hours ago. "My hair is untamable."

"I know," he said. She hiccupped and he didn't know why he found that endearing. He wished she wasn't in so much pain and blamed himself. He knew he could indulge the raw emotion tonight, but tomorrow, he'd put it aside and set a course to find out who was trying to destroy her business.

"You do know," she said. Zoe moved closer to the edge of the bed where he sat. "I wish we could start over. I wish that this awful business wasn't between us."

"No, don't go back there. You were almost asleep. I'm going to leave you alone so you can rest."

"Don't leave yet. I want you to stay. Lie down." Zoe moved over and made room for him.

"Zoe, I won't be helpful in the resting process if I'm in bed with you."

She felt her heartbeat speed up at the idea that he was going upstairs to his room and he'd leave her in this guest room downstairs. She pushed back the covers. "I look like chopped liver, Ben. You can keep it together. Please?" she asked, as if she knew proof positive of the words she spoke. Ben wished he had her faith. Because even in her vulnerable state, he still wanted her. That was the man in him.

His house was quiet and Zoe assumed his brothers were gone. Nobody was doing anything tonight.

"Don't blame me if I fall in love with you tonight," he said, removing his pants and shirt before climbing in.

Zoe slid her arms around his neck and hugged him. "How could I ever blame you for that? If you fall in love with me then that only means you were supposed to be with me. Especially with the way that I look."

He gently kissed her nose. "The sad thing is, Zoe, you probably won't remember this conversation tomorrow because you're under the influence of drugs and a concussion. So, I'm going to take all this affection, still do my job and take care of you."

"I want to remember this talk. I wanted you to know that I liked you. That the problem wasn't you, it was me. I know that's cliché." She yawned again. Ben curled around Zoe, waking her every couple of hours, standard concussion treatment. He awoke the next day, Rob's angry glare beaming down on him.

Chapter 8

"You were supposed to call and tell me her condition," Rob said, his voice well-controlled though angry.

Hood Team One consisted of Rob, Ben, Zachary and their cousin Hugh, the computer expert, and they were assembled in the dining room of Ben's house at nine o'clock in the morning to have a debriefing meeting.

Ben endured Rob's angry glare.

"I was going to call after I'd gotten her situated, but we didn't get home until three o'clock this morning. Zoe was in a state of vulnerability last night. She has a minor concussion, abrasions and two badly bruised ribs. In case you didn't know, we'd had a relationship prior to her becoming a client of this firm, and I want to add nothing happened last night. My first concern is her safety. I would never do anything to compromise that. Never. I stayed awake most of the night waking her up every hour and then dozed off to be awakened by you. Now that everyone knows, let's shift back to business."

Ben completed his report and loaded the electronic card with pictures of her bruises. They studied the bruise that had the ring insignia.

"Bring us up to speed as to why she didn't go to the police station? There are four between here and the mall," Zachary stated.

Rob held up his hand. "She's got quite a bit of money invested in an expansion. If she reports losses in terms of thefts—that have now escalated to assault—she will lose well over a million dollars in investment money and not get her two new stores."

"I feel as if we slept a perfect opportunity by letting this group hone their skills," Ben said. "I take full responsibility. I erroneously thought Faye and Martinez were the only perpetrators, and it's obvious that assumption wasn't true. My instincts say follow the money. We have to come back stronger than ever before.

"If you're not on a project, you're on this one. We need coverage for surveillance at the two stores, one at Galleria and one on Peachtree. She's got plans to open two more, but before she can open them, her theft numbers must be near zero. I'm pulling myself from surveillance and turning that over to Zach. I'm one hundred percent Zoe's bodyguard and in the ghost position. I'll be in charge behind the scenes only to be used as needed, until this is over."

Hugh, the quiet but studious Hood spoke up. "I've pulled her sister's financials and they're whack. She got suspended from her job two weeks ago because of the foreclosure, and the arrest will likely seal her fate at the bank. She had every reason to come after Zoe. Flint and Faye Clark asked Zoe to cosign on a loan last August. Zoe refused and referred them to a credit counselor. I'm sure that didn't go over too well."

"Excellent work, Hugh, given the notice," Rob told him. "Any word on where Flint Clark is?"

"He's engaged to an African princess pending his divorce. This is all in a letter on his credit report, if you can believe that." Hugh just shook his head. "The guy is crazy. He's suing his ex-wife for support and he'll likely get it because of the prenup they signed. He has a low probability of going after Zoe."

The men all shook their heads in disbelief.

Rob interrupted their straying thoughts. "Where's Zach? I thought he'd gotten back."

Zach walked in with a DVD in his hand. "I have the video of the altercation. I had to shake the hell out of the mall security guard to pull the damned thing. He wasn't even aware that she was in the building. It's grainy, but it's good enough to see what went on in that hallway. I'm warning you it ain't pretty."

Ben held his breath not knowing what to expect. He waited while it was loaded and watched the video. He tried to stay objective, but all he could see was a woman being beaten.

The fight didn't last longer than three minutes, but he was nauseous by the time it was over. "I'm going to kill whoever did this."

"I second that, but dude, she's a good fighter," Zach told him. "Zoe got away. That's a helluva lot more than a lot of women could have done. Look at the way she breaks his nose. I love it. Her elbows come up. One, two! Damn, that's sweet. That makes him easier for us to spot. A man with a broken nose and two black eyes. Beautiful."

"She did good, Ben. Make sure she knows that," Rob told him.

The words had extra meaning coming from him. Rob's wife had been killed and her killer was still on the loose. Ben knew Rob looked for the guy on his days off, although he denied it. But he would do the same and no one would be able to stop him.

Still, Rob's words were of little comfort when he thought about the bruises on Zoe's body all because of some jewelry.

"We've got to start from square one. What is Zoe's past and why would somebody want to hurt her?"

Chapter 9

Zoe dreamed she was in aquamarine water, purple and yellow fish swimming beneath her. She reached the white sandy shore and could hardly pull herself from the tranquil sea. Reaching out, she touched a foot as dry as the sand. It jerked and Ben's face came into view.

"You want some water?"

The offer seemed surreal, considering. She looked around. There were four walls and she was in a bed of white eyelet. Zoe exhaled slowly. "Yes, water. What time is it?" she managed, barely.

"Ten-thirty. I called Ireland, and Rob met her at the Galleria store, and Zach met Stacia at the Peachtree store. He opened with her."

"I'd better call them anyway." Zoe dialed both ladies and explained that she was ill and why they'd now have hand-some security men to help them.

Ben returned with the water, a cool cloth and a light breakfast. Zoe tried to move around in the bed but was caught up in the sheet and the T-shirt. She was accustomed to sleeping nude and struggled to find a comfortable place.

"My head still hurts. I think I'd better eat and take something. I'll feel better after a shower."

"Why not just chill in the bed for a while longer?"

"I'm used to being up at this hour. Since I can't go to work, I still need to be sitting up, even if it's only in the living room. My clothes—"

Ben stood in the doorway. "I can loan you some sweat pants and a T-shirt."

"I bought some stuff yesterday and my gym bag is in the car. I have a full set of clothes in there."

Ben smiled, showing how impressed he was. "I'll get your things. You eat and rest awhile longer."

Zoe nodded, but as soon as he turned his back, she headed into the bathroom to shower.

When she finished, she stepped out of the marble stall and swaddled herself in a warm towel. He had towel warmers. Everything about Ben's house was luxurious. Her head was hurting but as soon as she ate, she knew she'd start to feel better. Zoe made it back to the room and saw her clothes neatly laid out on the bed. A smile blossomed despite the pain in her head, and she dug in her gym bag for her set of toiletries and tried to decide on her clothes.

Ben had emptied both her gym and shopping bags. Three bras and her new boy shorts were on the bed, along with a cute thong she'd bought on impulse. Two pairs of black pants were laid out as well as a sleeveless summer dress and a skirt. She pulled on the underwear when there was a knock at the door.

"Can I come in?"

Zoe wrapped herself in the towel. "Okay."

Ben walked in and stood next to her. "Do you live in your car? You have clothes, enough canned food for a food drive and money in there. You just need a bathroom and you're set."

"If my head didn't hurt I'd laugh. I meant to drop that food off yesterday at church, but never got around to it. Ben, I don't know what to wear, so I'm going with the dress."

He shrugged. "Good choice, but you put on a bra and the dress is strapless. The problem is that the dress is nice, but it's a bit formal for sitting around. You have a lot of bottoms and no tops."

"Right," she whispered. "You choose."

He chose the black pants and pulled his green polo shirt over his head. "It's clean. I just put it on."

The shirt swallowed her, but she was comfortable. "Perfect. It's almost at my knees. What are your plans for the day?"

"I'm all yours."

"No," Zoe insisted. "You have to have something to do besides babysit me."

"Nope. We're together all day, so we're in the living room on the couch or here in the bed. Your choice."

"What about in the kitchen eating?"

His eyes brightened. "I like a woman with an appetite. I can cook scrambled eggs and I can burn scrambled eggs. Which do you prefer?"

"Oh, my. The choices."

Ben took her hand and started out of the bedroom. "Ben, I want to clean the room up first."

"We'll come back to it."

"You mean you will." They laced fingers as he guided her up the long hallway. "I went into the bathroom and took a quick shower, and when I came out you'd already made the bed and had my clothes laid out neatly. You can't spoil me like this."

"Why?"

"I might get used to it. When I get home I'll be looking for someone to be as nice and there'll be no one special."

"If you need any special treatment, I'm a phone call away. Sit down in the kitchen. I'm going to run upstairs and get a shirt. I'll be right back."

True to his word, Ben was back in a blue shirt that matched hers in design. He opened the refrigerator while she started the coffee maker. Suddenly tired, Zoe sat down at the marble counter on a stool and watched Ben cook.

Muscular and adept, he'd lied about his cooking ability. Within ten minutes, he'd made coffee, toast, grits, eggs and country ham. He served their food on gorgeous gold-lined plates, and Zoe grabbed the steaming mugs of coffee and followed him into the dining room.

They sat down at the table for eight and Ben prayed over their food and they began to eat.

"You're full of surprises," she told him, eating the fluffy eggs.

"Why?"

"You can cook. You pray."

He laughed at her. "You're an atheist?"

"No! I'm just surprised. Do you go to church, too?"

He looked at her slyly. "Will I get bonus points?"

"Not a single one. You can't bargain faith."

"Good answer," he said and finished chewing. "Yes, I go, but rarely."

Zoe nodded. "I go when I don't have to work. But lately I've been working a lot. That explains the canned food in the back of my car. I've been meaning to stop by and drop it off at the food bank."

"That's nice of you. I buy canned food and never eat it," Ben said, laughing.

Zoe nodded. "I had to check the expiration dates. I found some cans in my cabinet from two years ago. I tossed those out."

"You trying to give people ptomaine poisoning?" he asked, teasing.

"No," she answered, making it sound more like a question.

"That's really bad," he told her. "When do you cook for yourself? What do you eat?"

"There's this great service that allows you to go in and cook two-weeks' worth of meals at one time. Then you freeze them. Once a week I buy fresh greens for a salad and I'm good to go. I unfreeze the food and eat it."

Ben looked skeptical. "That sounds terrible."

"No, it's good food and it's fresh."

He looked at her plate and gestured with his fork. "This is fresh. That stuff you eat is frozen."

"Ben, you're missing the point of the program."

He shook his head. "No, I'm not. They're charging you a lot of money to make your own frozen dinners."

Zoe thought about it for a second and shook her head. "No, that's not true. Okay, we're making dinners and freezing them—"

"I rest my case."

Zoe ate a small piece of ham, but her head started a low throb so she put it down. "OK, Mr. Attorney. I don't know why you're smiling."

"You're so cute."

"I'm mad now," she said, trying not to laugh at his big grin. She picked up her coffee and sipped. "Shouldn't we at least stop by the stores?"

"No."

"What are you going to do all day?"

"Rest."

Ben got up and took their plates into the kitchen.

Zoe walked in and helped clean up and Ben let her. The sun had emerged after their second day of rain. Zoe was glad for the respite. When the kitchen was clean, she went back to her room and tidied up, then felt Ben behind her.

"What?" she asked.

"I ordered a movie on TV. Want to watch?"

"Sure. What is it?"

"A comedy with Sanaa Lathan."

Zoe followed Ben back to the living room which was like a theater, and sat on the couch by herself while he sat in a large easy chair. She wanted to sit with him, but she didn't want to act like they had to be together.

Although it was hot outside, it was cool in the house, and she crossed her arms and legs as the movie played. "Zoe, come over here."

She felt as if she'd been summoned by the teacher. "Yes?"

"Sit with me. I miss you."

Happy, she sat down and realized the chair was made for two. "You've been keeping this from me." Zoe crossed her legs so they were closer to Ben's. He got up and pulled a beautiful chenille blanket from a chest in a corner.

"Better?" She couldn't tell him how much better she felt. She just nodded. "I thought you knew," Ben said. "Besides, you were safer on the couch."

"How's that?"

"If I'd come over there, I'd have had you on your back making love to you." He looked at her over his shoulder and his hands caressed her legs. "Get closer."

"I'm practically molded to your back." She scooted over to give him more room. There was no denying the sexual attraction, but Zoe didn't want to substitute an opportunity to get to know Ben for sex. She'd already made that mistake once and had left, feeling like a fool.

"Are your mom and dad still alive?"

Ben shook his head no. "Dad died years ago and Mom, two years ago."

"So, it's just you kids."

"Yes, and we all get along. That's the nice thing about us. We genuinely love each other and look out for one another."

"That's why you're successful."

"We respect each other."

Zoe looked away from him. "I've never felt that Faye respected me. Maybe things would have been different if I'd have had a brother."

Ben shook his head. "He'd have tormented you."

She laughed. "How?"

"Boys bother girls. It's our job to push them and taunt them and in general make them miserable."

She sighed. "I had a sister for that. Who'd you make the most miserable?"

"Xan. She's the oldest out of all of us and we about drove her crazy, but Xan hit the hardest so we didn't bother her too much."

Zoe nodded. "I think I like her. What about Mel?"

"She's the baby and nobody messed with Mel. Besides, she's short."

"That's discrimination!"

He shrugged. "Call it what you want. We didn't bother her. She was young and little. She got away with murder."

"And now is she a brat?"

"No." He shook his head. "She's got two girls and one is deaf. She's on Hood Trap Team Two and is a martial arts expert."

"Wow. I really admire her. What's her day job?"

"She owns her own cleaning business. Yes, I'm one of her clients. She cleans my house and I pay full price," he declared.

Zoe laughed and they leaned back so that the chair was fully reclined. She closed her eyes and yawned. "You know I was about to ask. You're really racking up points, Ben Hood."

"What's that mean, Zoe McKnight?" He turned so that he was lying on his side and so was she. Ben tucked the blanket around her.

"That means if I wasn't sleepy and we were on that couch, we'd be making love right now."

"Can't you stay awake for twenty minutes?"

She snickered as he fingered the curls on her forehead and moved them out the way. "That's not enough time." Zoe burrowed close to him. "We'd need time to play with everything."

He kissed her forehead and the cheek with no bruises. "Play with what?"

"The pearls," she whispered.

"You received them."

Zoe kissed his neck. "I opened them before I left last night. I hadn't seen the mail until before I was about to walk out the door."

"I wanted you to come back to me." Ben put his hand on her waist and brought her closer to him.

"I had just made up my mind to come before I was attacked. Afterward, all I could think about was getting here."

"I wish under better circumstances."

"You had a date."

"That lady wasn't any date of mine," he said, nuzzling beside her nose, kissing her eyes and cheek.

"I hope you don't refer to me as *that lady*. That would hurt my feelings."

Ben massaged her bottom, but didn't make a move on her. "How should I refer to you?"

She shrugged and burrowed closer to him.

With his thumb he pushed her hair away from her eyes and leaned back so he could see her fully. "Tell me."

"I want to be someone's last first kiss."

Ben put his hand on her back and her heart beat as strong as a drum. He used to run from this conversation with women, knowing they wanted to get married and have babies. In his younger days he hadn't been ready. But as he lay in his living room with Zoe, he couldn't think of a way he'd rather spend his day.

"I want that same thing, Zoe. Maybe we're searching in the same waters. I think we might be."

She thumbed a tear from her eyes. "We might be," she agreed. "I'm not letting you pay for those pearl earrings."

Ben gently tugged on a curl and then tickled her ear with it, causing her to squirm. Zoe pressed her hand into her temple. "Ben, you're being bad. That's the most expensive date you never really had. I wore the pearls here but before I thought I'd lost them."

Her hands journeyed under his shirt to his abs of steel.

"Because when you wrapped them around me, they became a part of me. Since I can't wear them outside and tell people how I got them, you can at least enjoy the memory of our pleasure. Does it hurt if I touch your hip here?" He stroked her hip and bottom as his maleness pressed against her stomach.

"No," she said, breathless.

"Good, because that's as far as we're going. I'm not injuring you."

"The doctor didn't say anything about not making love," Zoe informed him.

"He didn't say anything about doing it, either."

Zoe pressed herself into Ben and kissed his lips. "Fine, if you want to waste a perfectly good erection." Within minutes her breathing evened out and she dozed off. Ben knew she was serious. As she slept, he watched her for at least a half hour. *Her last first kiss.* But he wondered if she could really understand how close his lifestyle was to her father's life as a cop.

Chapter 10

The medication took the edge off her headache, but left Zoe feeling drowsy. She dreamed of leaving work, frantic and scared out of her mind, running with her gun in her hand and driving with it in her lap. She'd been so afraid that she was being followed that she'd driven over the double-yellow line several times before calming her guttural gasps.

Every car that had pulled up beside her had been in danger—those poor people—but she'd kept her head and hadn't shown the absolute fear that threatened to rip her sanity to shreds: that the perpetrators were following her to finish her off. Her only thought had been to get to Ben, and when she'd scraped the undercarriage of her car hitting his driveway too fast, she hadn't cared.

Zoe woke up and realized she'd been crying in her sleep. She walked to the bathroom and washed her face and brushed her teeth, and found her gym bag and running shorts. She pulled on Ben's shirt and wondered what time of day it was.

Walking around the room she felt claustrophobic, and she was tired of being alone. The last thing she remembered was being in the living room with Ben watching a movie. He must have put her in the bed. Even though she felt weepy, she wiped her eyes, dabbed gloss on her lips and sighed. She needed to shake the memory of that dream.

Two tears fell and she dried her eyes as she opened the door. Zoe wished she could roll back the clock and chart a new, steadier course. She wasn't supposed to see Ben again, but karma had presented this anomaly, and had brought them together, and Zoe knew to pay attention.

She'd agreed to not begin anything with him, and she had to keep to her word. Truly, she was in no position to think of starting a relationship. But her body throbbed from being in Ben's presence.

The house was quiet, and she walked the cold floor to the refrigerator and chose a deep-red apple before looking for Ben, knowing from looking out the kitchen window that it was the middle of the night.

Funny that Ben didn't have any clocks. She had them everywhere in her house, but then again, she was time conscious. She took a small bite from the apple and savored its sweetness. Tiptoeing, she hurried up the stairs and walked past Ben's office to his room. She listened at the door and then knocked lightly. He didn't answer so she turned the knob.

Ben lay in bed on his side with his eyes open. Zoe walked over to him and leaned closer.

"You couldn't sleep?"

Zoe jumped. "I didn't know you were awake."

"I know when someone's walking around my house."

"I thought I was being quiet."

"No, I heard you. How are you?" He turned on the headboard light and dimmed it until the glow was a muted amber color.

"Weepy. I didn't want to be alone."

"You came to the right place. You want to lie down?"

"No. That's a little complicated."

He pushed up, his hand supporting his chin. "That's the point."

She smiled and sat on the bed, her back against the headboard. "You're a bad influence on me." She bit the apple again and offered him some. Ben bit and gave it back.

"Salty," he said.

"Tears, sorry."

"I tried to take good care of you."

"You're doing a great job." She reached for his hand and he brought it to his lips. Never one to shy away from pleasure, she didn't stifle the tingles as they ran up her arm and over her breasts. Ben brought her hand against his five o'clock shadow and before she knew it, she was in his arms lying next to him for an unexpected, rocking hug.

Despite everything she'd just said, she couldn't think of anywhere she'd rather be. This wasn't about business. This was personal, oh, so personal. "I just want to stay here for a little while."

"I'm not leaving you alone again until I'm comfortable you're safe. You're stuck with me." Ben used the ends of her hair to tickle her under her chin, and then they lay in silence, the unexpected rain their only backdrop of sound.

Zoe's heartbeat gentled to a pace that invited pleasure or rest. "Yeah?" she said.

"Yeah." His hand slid up her bare thigh and down again, and he pulled the covers up, cocooning her.

"Ben?"

"Yeah, baby?"

"I feel like I've been with you again. Have I?"

He shook his head no. "We've done a lot of talking and touching. I told you you wouldn't remember half of it, but we weren't together."

"Can I be honest with you?" she asked, her foot moving up his leg.

Ben nodded.

"I want to be. Is that just me being vulnerable or were we there beyond the touching?"

"We were there, baby." She looked as if she didn't quite believe him and he smiled. "You're going to know when we make love, Zoe. You're going to remember everything. Every time I really touch you and you really touch me. Every time my tongue tastes you and yours me, and every time you accept me into your body. Come closer."

Ben had her on her back and claimed her mouth in a slow drugging kiss. His lips caressed hers, his tongue tasting the sweetness of her mouth, leaving her lips tingling. Softening his assault, he massaged her breast, making her arch, her apple rolling away forgotten.

Slowly he released her. When she opened her eyes, he was grinning at her. "You did that on purpose."

Ben nodded.

"Why? So I'd remember?"

"So you'd have new memories. Good ones."

Zoe wrinkled her nose, smiling. "You're a bad man, Ben Hood."

"You keep telling me that, baby. Lie down and get some rest."

"I'm tired of resting. Where's the television?" Zoe sat up.

"Downstairs and in the office."

She looked at him as if she didn't believe him. "Why not in your bedroom?"

"Because bedrooms are for two purposes only. Sleeping and making love."

She blinked several times and looked around until he started laughing. "We don't have to do either. We can sit and talk. Talking is allowed."

"I'm so glad talking is acceptable." She giggled, and lifted her arms to braid her hair and winced. "Can you braid this for me? It's everywhere."

It was Ben's turn to look surprised. "Me? Braid? Hmm. I can try. Now you divide it into threes and over and under, right?"

Zoe nodded. "But not too tight."

"Where'd you get all this hair from?" he asked.

"My mother's side of the family. You see, my dad doesn't have any and Faye takes after that side. Mom cut hers and I've toyed with the idea. But I like it. It's just unruly sometimes."

"It's gorgeous. You shouldn't cut it, and I know men don't have a say in anything because we don't do a damned thing but want your hair long so we can run our fingers through it. I have sisters who have yelled at us about their hair for years."

Zoe nodded. "It's a woman's preference. If she wants to wear her hair short, a man shouldn't jump on her to change it. My ex hated my hair curly. He wanted me to get it straightened every week. I just didn't have time for that. And that led to many fights."

Ben leaned down and around, looking at her. "Why did you pick him?"

"We met when I opened my first store. I thought he was this handsome, regular guy that moved to the beat of his own drum. My friends were hunting high-powered, white-collar types and I wasn't looking at all. Then Charles appeared out of nowhere."

"How did he win you over?"

"He cooked for me."

Ben took the braid out and started over. "You're kidding?"

"No. He approached me in my store and we just started talking. He was regular and used regular language and wasn't into schmoozing. I think I was trying to buck my girlfriends—who were chasing money—rather than look for the best man. There were signs he wasn't right, though."

"There's always signs. What didn't you see?"

"He didn't own anything. No car, house, cat, dog. No relationship with his family. No friends, really, except the people at the restaurant and he'd just started there six months before. He had a little money, but I should have paid better attention. I fell in love and we got married. Six months later, the verbal abuse started, he lost jobs and it was downhill for six years."

Ben finished the braid and got back under the covers with her. Zoe turned to face him.

"What happened then?"

"We got divorced, I paid support for two years and I haven't heard from him since. I pledged to never marry again, and here I am. I haven't had a relationship since I got divorced. I've dated, but not a serious relationship."

"So, you got scared and left me three months ago because you enjoyed my company. Go ahead and tell me how sorry you are."

Zoe wiped her face and Ben caught her hand in his. "I got scared and ran." She squeezed her nose at him, but looked him in the eye. "That's what happened."

He took his other hand and rubbed the bridge of her

nose. "You always squeeze your nose when you're uncomfortable or embarrassed."

Zoe nodded. "I know. I can't help it."

"It's okay. You don't have to be embarrassed or uncomfortable around me."

Zoe looked into his eyes and wondered how much she could trust Ben with her feelings. She'd put her life into his hands, but the two were distinctly different.

"What are you thinking?"

She could feel him assessing her as if he were trying to read her mind. She couldn't verbalize what she was feeling. She wasn't even sure herself. "I'm not sure. Random thoughts."

"Spit it out, Zoe."

"You know so much more than me and you seem so much wiser and that scares me, Ben. You seem to have it all together. Like you get to decide what you and I want."

"And that makes you afraid that I'm going to do what?"

She wiped her face and he took her hands. "There's no hair to hide behind. Just tell me."

"That! You read me and know things. Emotionally, your job and you scare me just a little. Not enough to make me run away. I want to get to know you more. I'm tired of being scared so I want to know you. Tell me about you. You're thirty-five and not married. You're a good-looking guy as far as I can see. So why no wife?"

"I've never met the right woman."

"Maybe your expectations were too high."

Ben shrugged, his thumb caressing her hand. "I'm not worried. There was a girl once in law school and we were quite close to getting engaged, but things fell apart."

"What happened?" Irrational fear coursed through Zoe at the woman and what she almost had.

"She chose my best friend over me."

"Well, she's not so bright, is she?"

Ben threw his head back and laughed. "No, she's not."

"Where's she now?" asked Zoe.

He shrugged. "I don't know. I guess I'll find out at our ten-year reunion at Georgetown law."

She felt her eyebrows go up. "Prestigious. So, let's say I get into trouble. You could be my attorney?"

He grinned at her. "Depends on the trouble and if I want to get you out. What's in it for me?"

Zoe licked her lips thinking, and Ben tugged on her T-shirt. "That's a good start."

He claimed her mouth again. His lips were full of promise and moved over hers, his tongue tangling with hers in a sensual dance. Zoe stretched out beside Ben. "This is what I've been fighting against for so long. Why is being intimate so easy with you?"

"Because it's time," he said.

"Time for what?"

"Only you can answer that for yourself."

"Because I'm vulnerable?"

Ben lowered his forehead to hers. "Is that the only reason you're up here in bed with me?"

"No, but I didn't want to be alone either."

"I don't want to make love to you because you're a frightened woman. I want to because we both want each other," Ben said.

"I know."

"You're not there yet," he told her, seeming to know.

Zoe shook her head. "I have to be honest."

"There's nothing wrong with that except I want you so badly."

"I'll go back downstairs."

"You're staying right here. I'm getting to the point where I can't sleep without you. I was up here thinking about how I could come down there and crawl in the bed with you."

Zoe giggled and kissed his neck. "You're wonderful."

"You keep telling me that and I'll start believing it. Go to sleep."

Zoe sighed and her eyes grew heavy. She felt like swimming in the sea of tranquility again. The water was warm, like sitting with Ben had been, and she felt peaceful, then she looked up and saw the sharks.

Chapter 11

Zoe opened the door of her parents' ranch-style home and walked inside, the newspaper in her hand, her keys jingling. "Hey, I'm here," she called.

"Oh, it's you. Dad, your daughter is here," Faye called out.

Fred, her father's Norwich Terrier raced out of the back room and straight to Zoe. She bent down, dropping the newspaper and petted him. "Hi, Fred. How are you? You been a good boy? Ben, this is Fred. My father's best friend in the whole world."

"Hi, Fred," Ben said, petting the small dog.

"No, that would be you, the princess," Faye said derisively from the kitchen.

Zoe looked up at Ben, shaking her head. "Fred replaced me. I don't mind 'cause he's so cute. Aren't you, Fred?"

Fred barked and wagged his tail, making Zoe laugh.

Zoe unbuttoned her jacket and threw it on the woven-backed dining-room chair. "Ben, you want to take your jacket off?"

"Naw, baby. I'm good. Let's get this done so we can get to Zoe's at the Galleria. We said you'd do half a day today. Remember what the doctor said at your appointment this morning. Don't overdo it."

"Dr. Lara said I could go back to work after two days off. It's Thursday."

"Everything's under control, so why push it? You can review resumes for the new stores on the couch at the house."

"I'm going to win a discussion with you one day, Mr. Hood." Zoe headed into the kitchen. The yellow room was bright and sunny, marred by dishes that had piled up. "Where's Mom?"

Faye stared at her. "I don't see her so I guess she's not here. What the hell happened to you?"

"I was assaulted. Where's Daddy?" she asked her sister, who sat at the butcher-block kitchen table reading a popular magazine, oblivious to the dirty room. Their mother wouldn't abide this mess had she been there, so Faye was really being obnoxious.

Faye finally blinked. "I guess in his room or the bathroom. They're grown and don't need me to keep tabs on them, Princess Zoe. That sounds so cute. You ought to have a musical."

"Cut the crap, Faye. Your cynicism is unattractive. Do you have anything to say to me about what happened in the store? The two robberies you helped orchestrate?"

Faye looked up like she'd just seen Zoe for the first time that day. "No," she answered plainly.

"You don't think you should apologize? We're sisters."

Faye looked at her as if she'd lost her mind. "I'd buy that BS if we were on a reality TV show, but the truth of the matter is that we weren't ever close, Zoe, so you can cut the crap for your boyfriend here.

"You haven't lost everything you worked for all your life, and your husband didn't throw you over for another woman and then flaunt it all about town. I'm humiliated, and now you compound my humiliation by having me prosecuted. You couldn't have taken your jewelry back and just let me go, could you? I've lost my job because of you, so you can take your respect and get out of my face!" Faye sounded as bitter as she looked.

"Faye, you're tearing the family apart because you stole from me and you don't act remorseful. I feel—"

"Don't feel sorry for me," Faye yelled, shaking. "I don't need your pity."

Fred ran down the hall and hid. He didn't handle conflict well.

"I wasn't going to say that I feel sorry. I feel horrified that we're dividing the family, and that this is even happening. That I have to ask you questions about other attempts to hurt me and my business."

"I guess we reap what we sow."

"What does that mean?" Ben said, tired of Faye's disdain for her sister.

"Looks like somebody already expressed themselves quite well on her face."

"So I deserved to get attacked? Fine, Faye. I guess Daddy deserved to get run over." Zoe got up. "And you deserve what's happening to you. That's what your words mean."

Her father walked into the room. "Faye, shut up. You're not making any sense," he said, and poured himself some coffee.

"Dad, I'm sorry I can't stay. Ben Hood, my father, Anthony McKnight."

"No, I'm leaving." Faye tried to turn the attention back to herself. "He's the man that was nice enough to go through my purse and steal my earrings. Do I get those back?"

"You're hilarious," Zoe told her sister. "I have you on video taking them out the case and putting them on."

Anthony looked at his oldest daughter. "You can leave after you clean up this kitchen like you told your mother. She's out teaching at the community school and you're too old for me to be telling you to do things, Fayedra. I'm going to see your sister out, and then you and I are going to have a talk. *Then* you're leaving."

Zoe grabbed her jacket and followed Ben out the door. He held it open for her Dad who walked with an unsteady gait. Anthony whistled for Fred. The small dog zipped past them and onto the front lawn.

"You look like you fell off the top of the cheerleading pile," Zoe's dad said.

Zoe scrunched her nose at her father and kissed his cheek. "Be quiet, ya hear? I won. You should see the other guy. He's got a dislocated nose."

"Well, you finally learned something from all those boxing lessons I gave you."

Zoe cast a long-suffering look Ben's way. "My father likes to tell tall tales. He never gave me boxing lessons. He told me to crack an attacker over the head with a brick and go for the nuts."

Ben shook his finger at Anthony. "Good one. You should listen to your father."

"Dad, really, this happened at my store as I was leaving. I was attacked by a man and was able to fend him off well enough, but not before he got in a few hits."

"That's a shame." He shook his head. "I'm so sorry I wasn't able to help you, Zoe."

"Dad, I didn't come over here to make you feel bad."

"No, sir," Ben said. "Hood Investigations is on the case and we're taking good care of Zoe. Nothing else is going to happen to her."

"All right. I guess I got to trust somebody."

"Come on, we have to go. Dad, are you going to be all right with her?" They slowly walked down the long driveway and stopped at the street where Anthony pulled his mail from the mailbox.

"I'll be fine," he said. "Faye's got to leave. That may mess up the conditions of her bail, but that's her situation. It was nice and peaceful until she moved in. Now I've got to listen to her angry whining day and night to your mother. She's in a bad way, but she's making my blood pressure rise. I left East Point because I couldn't change anything, but I can change who I live with, that's for sure. That's why your mama works at the school three days a week. So I don't change her, too. Now about your face—"

"Dad, it's getting better. Ben Hood and the rest of his investigative team are working things out."

"Rob called me yesterday and gave me an update. Bet you two didn't know that, did you?"

They looked at each other surprised. "No," Zoe said. "I didn't know. But I'll thank him."

"We worked together once. He's a bright young man." Her dad looked at Ben. "You favor him a lot. He's better looking."

Ben burst out laughing and so did her father.

"Daddy!" Zoe admonished. He drew his hand back when Zoe tried to swat him.

Fred barked at her.

"That's right, Killer. Get her," Anthony said to his dog.

Ben and Zoe laughed as the dog ran up the long walkway to the front door.

"He's not much of an attack dog, Daddy."

"Not so much," her father agreed. "I don't miss anything that goes on in this house. Your sister is afraid and shocked that you had her prosecuted, but this subsequent attack—" her dad shook his head. "This isn't her."

Zoe nodded, looking at the ground. "If I hadn't done it now, she'd have done something worse later."

"When you were five and she was ten I told you to knock the hell out of her and you didn't. Now you want to get mad. The girl has a right to be confused."

Zoe gently bumped her father. "We're adults, now, Dad. It's a whole new ballgame. Go in the house before I really get you."

"As for you, Hood, I hope Zoe doesn't come back looking any worse than this. Her mother will have something to say once Faye and I tell her we've see how bruised up Zoe is."

Ben touched Zoe's chin and remembered how smooth her skin felt. "You have my word. The next time you see her, she'll be even prettier."

"My daughter doesn't trust just anyone, so don't disappoint me."

Ben shook Anthony's hand. "I won't."

Zoe kissed her father's cheek and they got into the car and started driving as Ben's phone started to ring. "Hugh, what's up?"

"Yo, Zach reported that the glass installer for the cases in Zoe's store didn't have a valid business license and he's closed up shop. Also, this is what made me call you. We set off the alarms in the Peachtree store and nothing happened."

"What do you mean nothing happened? Hold on. An ambulance is going by."

Ambulance sirens screamed as the large vehicles drove

by. Ben exited and took Ponce de Leon, running parallel with 85 North.

"The alarms didn't go off, man." The grimness of Hugh's voice finally made Ben understand what he was saying. "The sensors were made to look real, but they're not."

"Get on here and we can ride the HOV lanes to Lenox Road, Ben," Zoe told him.

He nodded, drifting down the on ramp. "I think we're in the middle of something big about to happen," Hugh told him.

"Nice," Ben surmised. "Call Rob and tell him to get ready to ride." Ben kissed Zoe's urgently pointing finger before saying, "Baby, I got this."

"Whoa, cowboy. *We're* riding," Hugh told him. "You're holding it down as ghost, remember?"

Ben had to stop himself twice, but he only had to look at Zoe once to remember he was her bodyguard, and his primary function was to keep her out of harm's way. "Got it. Zoe, when were the cases upgraded at your Peachtree store?"

"Three weeks ago. Brand new sensors and tinted glass. Why?"

"According to Zach and Hugh, the sensors aren't real. We're heading to Peachtree now. Be there in ten minutes."

"Ben, take care of Zoe. We can handle everything else."

Of course they could. "All right. Keep me posted."

Ben knew of a million ways he could entertain Zoe, and having her to himself, he decided they should have some fun.

Chapter 12

Traffic pressed in on Zoe's right filling her with a sense of claustrophobia. She pulled at her seat-belt strap, sat up and back in her seat then leaned left as if that would get her away from the cars. "I did everything you said. Talked about respect and ruining the family, and did Faye care, no! She's never going to change. I tried. That's all I have to say."

"I don't think she had anything to do with the attack, or she would have confessed. Everything she said today was emotional. You did this or that to her. She didn't mention the store or the jewelry. She'd have been only too glad to throw it in your face. She seems to be that kind of person."

"She is," Zoe admitted, hating his objective observation. "But she hates me. She wants to see me destroyed."

Ben kept shaking his head as he drove and Zoe wanted him to agree with her. Why was he being so rational? She rolled her eyes and wished she could get out of the car and walk so she could think. She played with the window lever then stopped, annoyed.

Oblivious, Ben talked about Faye. "She might hate you, but her first reaction was shock at your bruises, and then her features shut down. She didn't look victorious or superior, and she didn't look like she had a secret the way she did when I questioned her at the shop after the robbery. She isn't involved."

"But she still hates me." The thought still stung Zoe. The realization that she would never have a good relationship with her sister was a loss she hadn't expected. Ben and his family were all close. She'd thought he was going to argue more in his disagreement with Hugh, but all she'd heard was respect. That was a testament to the good relationship with his family.

The unmistakable sting of tears prickled her nose and she tried to fight them. "Oh, hell. No more crying. I need a better family. That's all."

"Why do you say that?"

"You were just disagreeing with Hugh, right?"

"Yes," he said.

"And you two didn't tear each other down. What you saw between me and Faye was Charles and me. That's why I don't ever want to get married again. I'm not sure how to have a healthy relationship."

"Let me ask you something," Ben said.

"What, Ben?" she said, exasperated.

"Why do you think that any man you've met or will meet in the future will be like your former husband? There's a lot of good men out there that don't want their women supporting them in that way. They don't verbally tear them apart just because they don't agree. They believe in taking care of their women and in working together, but you'll never meet that man because you've got this preconceived idea that what you had is all there is."

"The guy you're speaking of is one is a million. You may be the only one, Ben."

He leaned toward the driver's window and shook his head. "You should add some diversity to your life to counteract your negative low-grade hostility."

"What is low-grade hostility?" she asked, frustrated.

"You're not ready to pull a knife, but you would bang on the hood of the car if we weren't driving."

"Why is it that a woman can't get angry and voice her opinion without it being labeled low-grade hostility?"

"You're in my car, I'm not shouting, but your hands are on your hips and you're shouting and glaring at me. Hostile. Case closed."

He smiled at her and looked back at the road.

So what if he was right? She wanted to twist his perfect ear off. "I said I didn't want to talk about this. This is the very reason I don't need a man. You're always making snap judgments based upon one set of circumstances."

"Now, about getting rid of that hostility. Tell me one thing that you do besides work to relax."

"I take karate classes."

His sidelong look told her she couldn't count that.

"I read."

"You read magazines about jewelry. Who are your girlfriends and what do you do when you hang out?"

"I'm too busy. My best friend Loren moved back here a few years ago, but she's a bit of a recluse. I don't really go out. I've been working a lot."

"So how did you come to be hooked up with me?"

"I don't want to talk about that."

"Why not? We're stuck in a traffic jam. We're not going anywhere."

"I met your friend Terri Pritchard and she introduced us at the White Linen party. You bid on the Acapulco vacation and I couldn't let you win because I wanted it. And as they say, the rest is history."

"What did you report back to Terri about us?"

"I don't kiss and tell."

Ben leaned on the arm rest. "You didn't tell her it was the best sex of your life?"

"No, I didn't say that." She felt his fingers on her chest and realized he wasn't even touching her.

"It wasn't the best sex of your life? Before you answer, recognize that my ego is at stake." She watched him for several long seconds, cocooned in BMW black leather. Hood men weren't shy about their talent. He knew he'd been good. She'd wanted him all night long. Every time she'd moved last night so had he. She hadn't slept much at all.

"We can move up," she told him, hoping to deflect the conversation.

Ben glanced away from her, rolled two feet and pressed the brake. When his gaze returned, it was as intense as before. "Was it the worst?"

Ben was so close his breath slid down her neck, and reminded her of how it felt when he had her hanging off the side of his bed, his body completely attached to hers. "It was very nice."

Thankfully, the traffic began to move. Slowly, they crept past a shiny apple-green PT Cruiser that had met an unfortunate end against a barely ruffled 1985 Pontiac Bonneville.

A twentyish-looking woman sobbed into her cell phone—her hand flailing about with the citation she'd just been given—while a senior citizen and a cop were on the side of the road, watching the wreckers remove the women's vehicles from the roadway. "I don't use a sex-ometer, but it was good," Zoe lied.

"That's not what I wanted to hear," Ben told her. "I look at everything as a challenge. In the end, I win. It's like you've given me a C on a term paper."

The cars stopped again and Zoe pushed her purse onto the floor, then shoved it aside with her foot. The sex had been amazing and if he touched her thigh, she'd be wide-legged in the backseat. Yet, she wasn't ready for a relation-ship. Ben's house said he wanted to settle down. What man owned a four-bedroom house that didn't want people to live in them?

"Ben, we have something, but my focus has to remain on my work. Besides, what we had was really good. It's something we can't duplicate."

"That's over. We have something different, and you know it."

"It's only because of proximity and opportunity, don't you think? I'm not a booty-call kind of girl."

"I'm not stepping to you like that, so don't put me in that category. Got it?"

Zoe felt like she'd gotten her hand slapped. "Yes."

With a slight tug on her braid, he pulled her to him and claimed her with a smoothness that quelled all the lies she'd just told. His mouth moved over hers, teasing her, re-minding her of last night's kisses.

Ben's tongue played along her bottom lip and he kissed her right under her chin.

Zoe groaned and a sizzling tingle that couldn't be sup-pressed wiggled through her body. She didn't realize that she was cupping his face and leaning into the kiss until the car behind them reminded them they were on the road.

"Ms. McKnight, you make me forget myself."

What in the world am I doing? Zoe asked herself.

Ben hit the gas and guided them off the next exit to a vacant lot and looked Zoe straight in the eye. "Do you trust me?"

"Yes. Why?"

"I want to show you something special and I need your cooperation."

"If this is a joke where you show me something obscene—"

"Would I do that?" He got very close to her. "Trust me. Say yes."

"Yes."

He smiled, and kissed the beginning of the smile on her lips. "You're gorgeous."

Ben made her feel like she was in high school and in love again for the first time. Zoe looked out the window to try to gather her feelings that had scattered like pollen.

"Rob, it's me and Zoe. I already told Hugh that we weren't coming to the Peachtree store, but we're going to take two additional days off," Ben said into his phone.

Zoe looked at him surprised. "Yes, our phones will be on, and we'll be available at all times. She's getting stronger every minute. She had a follow-up appointment this morning. And the doctor said she's good to go, but to take it easy. Let's check in tonight. Sure we can." He pressed the Off button and put the phone in the holder.

Zoe touched Ben's arm. "I can't take another day off. I have a meeting coming up with the mall owner, Mitchell Turner, next Monday. I've got to be ready. Then I have to meet with designers in St. Thomas in two weeks. I've still got to hire staff for the new stores."

"You'll be at your meeting next week so stop worrying.

Two weeks is a long time away, so don't worry, you'll be there. You're going to have fun and get away from all this or I'm adding on the weekend."

"Ben, this is kidnapping." Her heartbeat thundered at the possibility of being with him four more days in a row. Being with him for three days had caused her to open up like a can of beans and tell all her secrets—her struggles with her ex-husband and with her sister, her loneliness, the fact that she didn't really have any friends besides Loren. No one knew those private difficulties except Ben.

She had already entrusted him with her professional safety, and now her personal freedom was in his hands.

He turned the car around and parked in the lot of a vacant building.

"I'm going to show you how much fun you can have, and we're going to find out who's robbing you. Believe it or not the two can happen at the same time."

"No, they can't. Ben, I insist you take me to my store and let me get my work done. I'm paying you."

"Zoe, your work is getting done and your bill is paid in full. I won't chance you getting hurt again. I'm protecting you. All of you. I'd feel personally responsible if you were to get hurt, so I'm going to make sure that doesn't happen again, so come on, let's go."

"Where are you taking me? We're in a vacant lot."

Ben just shook his head. "It's an unpaved parking lot. You've got to be more aware of your surroundings. We're going over there."

Zoe looked over her shoulder suspiciously, and her stomach did a triple axle, back flip and somersault when she saw the Ferris wheel.

Chapter 13

With her gaze focused, Zoe aimed her toy water gun at her horse and rider. The last bets had been placed and the cheering from the sound box, along with the real crowd behind her, filled the air. "You sure you don't want to quit while you're ahead?" Ben asked, taunting her.

"You scared, Hood? I've smoked you on the two games before this, and you're about to get beat again."

"Your overconfidence is adorable, McKnight," he shot back. "You already owe me two home-cooked meals and a Slushie for being a sissy for not riding the Ferris wheel."

"A girl can't be a sissy, and so what, anyway? I'm a master at this shooting game. Let's go double or nothing."

"I'm a smart investor. Doubling the bet is silly. I say we make it more interesting. It will cost you kisses. Two long, slow kisses at the time of my choosing."

"Shooters take your mark…" the announcer said, his pistol in the air.

Zoe's dark eyes danced. She loved a dare. Ben vowed to remember that. "You'd be breaking your own rules, Hood. Besides, once I win, you'll be cooking for me."

"You can bargain something else. I'm keeping my prizes. In fact, I want you to cook in the nude."

"No way!" Zoe yelled over the crowd, popping up from behind her water gun to glare at him. "You can't change the rules in the middle of the game. That's not fair."

"Get set," the announcer yelled.

"Okay. Wet T-shirt," Ben replied, loud enough for everyone behind them to hear. The men in the crowd roared.

Ben held his position, staring at the hole on the side of the horse's behind.

Zoe was already a lovely golden brown, but when she blushed, her cheeks turned to sunburned red. He wanted to eat her up.

"You set me up!"

She tried to pinch him, but he shrugged her off. "You fell for it."

"Go!" The fake pistol went off and Zoe started firing. Water squirted from her gun, missing the target completely. Ben laughed as his guy galloped closer to the finish line, while hers limped near the start line. Zoe tried hard to bump him.

"I don't think so, beautiful. Come over here again and I got something for you."

Zoe lost easily. Ben won the support of all the guys behind him. He collected the tickets that streamed from his machine and accepted his high-five congratulations. He made his way back to Zoe after choosing a furry dog as his prize.

"Where's my prize, lady?" he asked, snaking his arm around her shoulders, her braid caught beneath his arm. Her mouth was in the perfect kissing position.

"Oh no, buddy. When you invented the prize for the loser, I didn't agree to it. I'm not kissing you in the middle of this carnival."

"Why not? You bet me here. 'I'm gonna win, Hood. I'm the best at air hockey.' And you lost. Two games. Okay, Hood," he said, mimicking her. "I'm gonna squash you at the motorcycles."

"That's not fair. You didn't tell me you used to race motorcycles."

"You didn't ask for my extracurricular activity resume. I told you Hoods do a little bit of everything."

"In all fairness, we're supposed to be keeping this strictly business."

"That's correct, but we're not on a business trip, not in business clothes, and we're not in a business frame of mind. So, technically, we're two friends having fun, and I'm just trying to collect on a debt."

"May I ask you something?" Zoe said, flirtatiously.

People streamed by, oblivious to them standing in the middle of the carnival road, his arms wrapped around her neck, his chest against hers. "Yes."

"Do you kiss all your debtors? Because if you do, you might have some type of tongue cooties or something I need to know about right now."

"You're hilarious. Come here."

He kissed her right then, with a passion that grew in intensity. She didn't resist, but drew away first and when he opened his eyes, she was smiling.

She looked at him for a long moment and then her eyes got big. "Oooh. Funnel cakes."

He couldn't help but laugh. Where had that come from?

Zoe started digging in her purse for her wallet. "I'm buying you one of these. Have you ever had one?" She glanced over her shoulder at him, moving with childlike energy. She kept popping up on the toes of the black sneakers he'd bought her on the one pit stop they'd made before entering the carnival.

She'd already been wearing a snug pencil skirt that came to her knees, with her pink-colored wrap that was form-fitting to her body. Her hair was still braided, but the curls were as irreverent as she was, and several ringlets were now loose, and framed her face.

The markings of the attack were evident even with makeup, but she'd relaxed so much her beauty outshined the shadowy evil that had befallen her.

"Ben, did you hear me?"

"No, I don't want anything to drink."

"Okay, two funnel cakes with lots of powdered sugar and one blue, no, red Slushie." She turned around. "I don't welsh on my bets."

"I can't tell you how happy that makes me."

Zoe paid and took the funnel cakes. "Grab the drink, okay? Let's sit over there."

She pointed to some picnic tables that had been set up under a tent. The sun was relentless, and it was hard to believe that Zoe wasn't complaining about the heat.

But she hadn't ever complained about anything, Ben realized.

He sat down next to her. "Are there special eating instructions for these things?"

She shook her head and he saw her moving in slow motion. Her beauty captivated him. She had pretty white teeth, plump natural lips that she chewed when she was nervous or excited. Full, unblemished cheeks he wanted to stroke so often, and had to force himself to not think about, and eyes that were often more worried than a woman her age needed to be. He loved the bold jewelry she wore, how it enhanced her features and made her stand out. Zoe's sense of style made her sexier than any woman he'd ever known.

Her tongue darted around her lips in anticipation. "No instructions." She glanced at him with carefree eyes. This was so much better than the fear and worry he'd been seeing.

"You just bite and enjoy."

She raised her funnel cake and bit. Her head fell back, a huge smile on her face as she chewed. Powdered sugar covered her lips and chin. "This is heaven," she told him, licking sugar from her fingers.

How could he resist that endorsement? He bit into his and chewed, waiting for the moment when the celestial choirs would start singing. But nothing happened. It tasted like a hot, dry, crusty waffle. He couldn't tell her. She was enjoying hers too much.

The funnel cake turned into a big doughy ball in his mouth and he chewed, wanting to swallow.

"Don't you just want to die?" she asked him.

He nodded, his eyes tearing. He couldn't make any more saliva.

Zoe bit hers again and he watched her, loving the way her neck moved as she swallowed. The way she unconsciously lifted and turned her chin, then bumped her hair with her shoulder just to get it out of the way. Watching her was like watching Carlos Santana play the guitar.

He reached for the Slushie and relieved his tired jaw, swallowing the paste he'd made.

"Oooh, can I have some? I promise I don't have any mouth cooties."

"You still got jokes? You weren't worried about cooties a few minutes ago."

"Are you one of those types, Ben? You forget nothing? You remind your past loves—" she got off the table. "Lovers," she said, then fixed it again. "Flings of everything?"

"We kissed about ten minutes ago. It wasn't like it was yesterday, and yes, and only when it's worth remembering. Come on, it's time to ride."

"No, I don't like the rides."

"You've got a green belt in karate. You're not scared of anything."

He threw away his funnel cake and Zoe stopped short, looking in the can. "You didn't like it?"

"It was delicious. I don't want to spoil my appetite for dinner."

"You should have told me. I'd have saved it for you. I could have wrapped it up and put it in here with these guys. They wouldn't have minded."

She showed him her purse and the heads of three stuffed animals stuck out. He took her hand and she didn't pull away.

"Come on, a few rides, and then we'll go."

"Ben, I'm not a rider. You go and I'll watch."

"We don't have to do the water rides."

"I wasn't doing those anyway." She lagged, slowly. "I don't mind watching."

"Are you scared of hurling? I've seen men hurl before."

Zoe put on her best serious face. "You will never, as long as I live, see me puke my guts up, okay?"

"You're adorable." He stopped himself from kissing her again. "We'll do the teacups. What woman can resist the teacups? Even little girls are in line for the teacups."

Ben stuck his finger in the waistband of her skirt and guided her over.

"How old are you, sweetie?" He asked the little girl in line ahead of them who stood with her mother and father.

She looked at her mom who nodded before she answered him. "Seven, and my sister is four."

Zoe gently kneed him in the hamstring and Ben pretended not to notice. "My friend here is a little scared."

Both girls looked at Zoe with wide blue eyes. "It's just teacups," the older girl said.

"I know. Thank you," Zoe said, trying not to strangle him.

The little girl looked at her. "Just hold your daddy's hand. That's what I'm doing."

All of the adults burst out laughing.

Ben shrugged like he hadn't done anything and Zoe tickled his hand with her fingernails. "You're in for it later." She then extended her hand to the mother. "Hi, I'm Zoe, and this is Ben."

The woman turned around as the line moved up to the comfort of a wide shade tree. "Nice to meet you, Zoe. I'm Sweden and this is my husband Gordo, short for Gordon. Our girls, Emily and Hannah."

"Your girls are adorable." Zoe started, and pumped Ben's hand. Her voice was unusually high. "Sweden, that's a beautiful necklace. The stones are lovely. Amethyst and aquamarine, right?"

"Yes," she said, excited. "The other stones are citrine and garnet. You know your gems, Zoe. I absolutely love this piece."

"I do, too. I'd love for Ben to get one for me. Where'd you get it?"

"Gordo bought it for me for our tenth anniversary two weeks ago, but to be honest, I haven't seen this anywhere. He saw it online and met up with the seller in person, right, honey?"

"I did. We'd better move up."

"It's so unique. Reminds me of a collection I had in my store, Zoe's on Galleria."

"You're Zoe?" Sweden asked. She practically jumped in the air. "I *love* your jewelry. This silver you're wearing is so bold and sexy. Can I pull this off?" She touched Zoe's earrings and admired her bracelet.

Zoe nodded. "There's a look for every woman."

Sweden's expression said she was convinced. "Honey, I've got to visit Zoe's store. Ben, are you in the jewel business, too?"

He eyed Gordo. "No. I'm in the investigative business."

Gordo's smile faded and he looked uncomfortable. "I'm going to hit the restroom, honey. Watch the girls."

"Mommy, Daddy always has to potty when it's time to ride the teacups." Hannah looked disappointed at her father who was now jogging, and pulling out his cell phone.

Ben gave Zoe the eye and she seemed to understand. "Honey," she groaned, playing along. "Not you, too. I reminded him to go after lunch."

Hannah stomped her sandaled foot. "Boys."

Zoe rode the teacups twice with Sweden and her girls before Ben and Gordo returned. They exchanged a few more niceties with Sweden giving them their e-mail addresses and phone numbers much to Gordo's chagrin. Then the family departed in the opposite direction.

"What'd you find out?" The carnival crowd had thickened and Zoe had gotten some sun, making her look healthy. The bruise on her chin had been covered by makeup that was nearly worn off, but it didn't matter. She was still beautiful, but more than anything she was calm.

"He's a VP at a car dealership on Cobb Parkway, and he was very nervous that you were so interested in the necklace. Sweden's right. He did buy it online, but it was a private sale and he picked it up from a woman named Zoe. He paid two thousand dollars for it."

"Two grand? It cost five thousand dollars!"

"He thought I was going to take him down in front of his family, that's why he went to the bathroom. He was calling his attorney. I let him know I wasn't after him but would be contacting him very soon. I was only interested in the necklace and who he got it from. He gave up the information right away. You'll be surprised."

"Who? Tell me." Zoe had grabbed his hands and Ben knew he was going to raise her anxiety.

"He said he bought it from a woman named Zoe McKnight."

"That's me!" Stunned, Zoe looked up at him. "Do you think they're trying to take over every aspect of my life? How far-reaching is this?"

"I don't know, but I don't want you to panic. We're getting closer to finding the answers. Right now you're safe. Your stores are taken care of and everything is under control."

She finally nodded. "I have to admit you're right. I just freaks me out that there's someone out there trying to impersonate me."

"I know, but we'll shut them down. Let me call Hugh with this development and then we move on, okay?" Ben knew she wouldn't agree at first, but he'd come to know that and so much more about Zoe.

They headed toward the car and Ben held Zoe's door. "Where to, your majesty?"

"I want to go home and eat some real food," Zoe said. "Then put my feet up."

"Let me take you out to eat."

Zoe shook her head. "I eat out all the time because I

work in the mall. I never get to cook for anyone. Can we just go back to your house and eat? I still owe you a meal and possibly, possibly," she said in the softest voice, "a kiss. I might be willing to share half of that kiss now. As a down payment on later."

Ben grinned. "What is half a kiss? I don't think I've ever had half of a kiss."

"It's this." Zoe pressed her lips against Ben's, then slid her mouth to his neck, where she did everything she wanted to do to his mouth.

"You're a terrible woman," he said, running his hands over her breasts and hips.

"No fair," she breathed. "I'm teasing you."

"I guess we're both driving each other crazy."

Zoe kissed his nose and his lips. "Let's eat, then pick up where we left off."

Chapter 14

Zoe watched the pots on the stove, making sure the frying chicken and the beans were cooking at the proper levels. Ben had gone upstairs to shower and get an update from Rob, but had promised to be down in less than thirty minutes. Zoe had raided the pantry and refrigerator coming up with little that would make a decent meal. She needed salad and dessert and she knew exactly where to get it.

Dialing the phone, she waited for her best friend Loren to answer. She was the most amazing dessert chef in the world, her confections an undiscovered talent of the former model. Zoe had been trying to bring Loren out of her shell and her house, to no avail. But she hoped Loren would make her something special in honor of her evening with Ben. Loren finally answered the phone in her distinct Lakota Indian and English accent.

"Hey, how are you?" Zoe asked.

"Zoe," she said, surprised. "I'm fine, and you?"

"I'm good. I have a favor to ask. Please don't say no."

"If it's a date, no. If it's a double date, no."

"Good," Zoe giggled, knowing of Loren's distrust of men after her last boyfriend badly disfigured her, ending her modeling career. "I wouldn't dare. I need you to bake me a nice dessert. I've met someone and we're at his house. He's helping me with…a problem."

"Are you in trouble?" Loren sounded concerned and scared. "Don't trust him. He could be the problem."

"No, Loren," Zoe said, to put her mind at ease. "He's helping me, really. I trust him. I wanted to make a nice dessert, but I don't have a box cake mix."

"Zoe McKnight, did you say *box cake mix?* I ought to cut off your lips." The women shared a laugh. "I'll help you only if you promise that he's a good man and taking good care of you."

"He is, Loren. I need another favor. Can you deliver the cake to his house?"

There was a long silence and Zoe held her breath, turning down the fire under the two pots on the stove while she talked. "I'm not allowed to drive at the moment, so I can't pick up the cake."

"Okay, but I can't stay," she said, sounding a little tense. "What's the address?" Zoe knew what a sacrifice Loren was making. Though she made desserts for two restaurants, she rarely left her house anymore. And nothing Zoe said could get her to come out. She gave Loren the address and thanked her oldest friend.

"Hey?" Loren said before Zoe could hang up.

"What?"

"What else are you serving for dinner?"

"Fried chicken and beans," Zoe said, feeling as embarrassed as she sounded.

Loren made an unladylike sound into the phone that made Zoe laugh aloud.

"In my own defense, I'm at his house and that's about all Ben has. No potatoes, no rice, no grits, no eggs. We ate eggs for breakfast. He's a bachelor, Loren. What can I say? We need a salad."

"That's sad. I just catered a birthday dinner for the owner of the restaurant I bake for. He could have asked his chef, but he wanted me. I still have a lot of food left over. I can bring that, if you'd like."

"You are wonderful, Loren. I love you." Somehow Zoe knew her friend was smiling.

"I love you back, Zoe. I'll see you in an hour."

Zoe turned the chicken and covered the pots, then hurried down the hall to the bathroom to straighten up. Just as she'd predicted, Ben had already cleaned up everything, including her room. She showered and changed, glad that she kept such a well-stocked gym bag, then folded her dirty clothes so she could take them home.

Thinking of her house brought on a wave of homesickness Zoe hadn't expected. She'd been on ten-day vacations and hadn't missed her house or job, but for some reason, knowing she was mere miles away made her want to go home to be amongst her things.

She pushed a headband onto her head, then added her accessories: earrings, necklace and bracelets. Makeup followed and she hurried up the hallway and stopped short, surprised to see Rob and Zach, though she'd never met Zach formally.

"Rob. I didn't know you were here. I mean…I wasn't expecting you."

Rob came down the remaining stairs, a smile on his face. "Zoe, forgive the intrusion. We saw the lights on and came to check things out. Once we saw Ben's car, we decided to give him a quick update. Zoe, this is our younger brother, Zach."

Zachary was the biggest of the Hoods. As big as the Hulk, except he was the black version. His eyes lit up and a wide smile parted his lips exposing a gap between his top two teeth. Zoe immediately knew he had a playful demeanor. "It's nice to meet you, and under better circumstances," she said.

His handshake was that of a gentle giant. "Zoe, I've seen your work. I'm a big fan."

She looked at Rob, then back at Zach as she touched her spiral earrings. "You like my jewelry?"

"Yeah, that's nice, but when you broke that man's nose—" he put his hand to his heart "—I fell a little in love with you."

Rob glared at his brother, and Zoe burst out laughing. "Thank you, I think."

Ben bounded down the stairs. "You're both leaving, and Zoe and I are about to eat the dinner that's not going to burn because you're distracting her."

"Goodness!" She ran into the kitchen in time to save the chicken. Cutting off the pots, she removed the food and went through the cabinets in search of plates and utensils. She heard the men talking, the front door opening and closing, then their voices faded. Zoe wanted the dinner to be nice because her day with Ben had been so wonderful. But she couldn't help feeling just a little guilty for not offering to feed the very men who were taking such good care of her while she recuperated.

Being with Ben all day had given her an unquenchable desire to know him better, but she wasn't without manners. What was a few hours? She could learn a lot about Ben from watching him with his family. Her phone rang as she stuck the chicken in the warmer. "Hey, Loren. Where are you, honey?"

"Outside. This huge oaf is leaning on the hood of my car asking me to marry him. Get him off!"

"That's probably Zach," Zoe said, clenching her teeth as she grinned. "Ben," she called. "Is Zach outside?"

"Yes. Why?"

Zoe looked around, hearing him but not seeing him.

"I asked my friend Loren to make a dessert for me and she's here. Zach's playing with her and she's not the playful type. Can you help her?"

"I'll be right down."

Zoe looked in the foyer. "Where are you?"

"Upstairs. We came back up to the office for a minute. Zach ran to the car to get video from the Galleria store from today."

"Rob, would you like to stay for dinner?" Zoe said on impulse.

"No," Ben said.

"Yes!" Rob answered. "That would be nice. Thank you." He sounded as if he'd been waiting for her to ask the question.

"Zoe, we were this close to getting rid of them." Ben sounded like he was pouting. "Why'd you do that?"

"Guilt," she whispered, giggling. Her cell phone rang again. "They're working so hard and we were kicking them out. I cooked a whole pack of chicken and a pot of beans, and it's just you and me. Now please go get Loren before she drives away with the food."

"You sound cute even over the intercom."

"You're biased, but thank you. Loren," she reminded him.

"On it," he said, coming down the stairs and ducking into the kitchen.

Realizing they were alone, Ben backed her into the refrigerator, his hands seizing her waist. He slowly dragged his nose up her neck and Zoe squirmed. "You got a tan out there today," he said.

She touched her neck to hide the blush. "You had me out there at high noon. That's optimum roasting time." She arched and he leaned, their bodies connecting. Zoe's smile was quick, his, too, as he grabbed a handful of her ass. "Quit, and rescue Loren."

"I'm only into saving you."

Her body reacted with wanting as her lips parted and her hand snaked up his chest. Her fingers found their way into his mouth, and he licked them before claiming her lips.

She could hardly catch her breath from wanting him so badly, but she made herself pull away. "Stop before we get into something we won't have time to finish."

"We could finish it if you hadn't invited them to eat." He kissed her cheek and headed out when they heard the ruckus. "You're mine, you know that?"

"No, I don't."

"You still don't believe me?"

"No," she whispered.

"I'll show you later." He tapped the tip of her nose.

"I didn't mind asking Loren." Zoe scooted around Ben. "She needs to get out more. I want to comb my hair before we sit down and eat, but let me help her get everything inside first."

"Your hair looks fine, and I'll help her."

"That's okay. Ever since I washed it the ends feel ratty. Ben, I need to go home. I need my conditioner. My stuff."

"Non-negotiable right now."

"Fine, we'll talk about it later." Zoe acted as if she hadn't heard him. "The chicken is done."

"You're crazy!"

Zoe heard the explosive declaration from Loren before she entered the kitchen and set three trays on the island. Ben stood at attention, seemingly awed by Loren's obvious beauty.

She'd been a model years ago, but she'd let her hair grow long and wild, wore no makeup, put on ten pounds, and all it had done was enhance her exotic looks.

"You're harassing me, Zachary. Now stop." Loren was Lakota Indian and Black American and had never lost the accent she'd learned from her mother.

She was accustomed to having her orders followed. Zachary didn't seem to notice that he was bothering her.

"Why won't you marry me?" Zach asked.

"I've known you for three minutes and you're driving me nuts. Zoe, here's the food. I'm going home."

Ben and Zach looked from one to the other without saying a word. Zoe hadn't thought complete silence was possible, but Loren often had that affect on people.

"Please stay for dinner." Zoe offered.

"No."

"Loren," she chided. "You're being rude. This is my friend, Ben Hood. You met his brother, Zach, and Rob is somewhere around. I'd like you to at least say hello to the people who've been helping me."

Though they greeted her warmly, nothing about Loren's demeanor inspired conversation. She was different when it was just the two of them in her house, but ever since the attack two years ago, she'd changed, and hardly ever interacted with people anymore. She didn't make eye contact with any of them.

Loren said something in her native language and came around the island and looked at Zoe closely. "Do you want to come home with me?"

"I don't know where Rob is," Zoe told her, who seemed more uncomfortable than anything. "He's Ben's twin."

Loren was obviously ready to go, but Zoe was so glad to see her, and she'd hoped that Loren would stay a few minutes longer. "Loren, you thirsty?"

"No, Zoe. Walk me out, okay?"

"I'm back." Rob called. They could hear his keys hit the glass table in the foyer. "Everything in here smells delicious." He entered the kitchen and his gaze zeroed in on Loren.

"Rob, this is Loren, my best friend. She's on her way out."

Nobody moved and Zoe didn't understand their silence. These were good-looking men and she was sure they'd seen a beautiful woman before, but for some reason, they were transfixed, as if they all had a secret.

"Loren," he said softly, "Like Sophia Loren, the great actress?"

Loren nodded but didn't look at him. "Right."

Zoe gasped. This was the first time Loren had actually spoken to a man and didn't sound cross with him.

"Your eyes are green, aren't they?" Rob asked her. "My wife's eyes were green, too. She passed away."

Loren looked at him for a whole second. She took Zoe's hand. "Sorry for your loss."

The words seemed so hard for her to say, but sincerely meant. Ben stepped forward as if to console her. "It's okay," he said.

Loren pulled Zoe. "I've got to go home. Good night."

"She wants to marry me, Rob, so step aside." Zachary made the ridiculous statement and everyone looked at him.

Loren slow-blinked Zoe, letting her know she'd reached her threshold.

"Shut up," Ben told him quietly. "Thank you for the food, Loren, I'm sure we're going to enjoy it," Ben said.

A chorus of thank-yous followed them out.

Zoe and Ben walked Loren to her car, and she didn't recoil when Ben touched her hand when she got in. "Goodbye," she said quietly, and drove away.

Rob watched from the door.

"What's her story?" Ben asked.

Zoe waved until Loren's vehicle was out of sight. "She was maimed by a former boyfriend and it ended her modeling career. She's a near recluse now. Tonight was a rarity. I'm just glad she came out. It's the first time I've seen her in months."

"What happened to the boyfriend?" Rob asked.

"He got away with it."

"Tell her we will try to help her."

Zoe smiled. "I'll let her know."

Back in the house, Zachary rested his chin on his stacked fists. "Tell her I'm sorry for messing with her."

"I'm sure she knows you were just goofing off. No harm done," Zoe told him, and as promised, gave him the biggest piece of chicken.

"We're going to get your case solved expediently, Zoe," Rob said, his demeanor businesslike.

"Thank you, Rob. Can we serve dinner? The food is hot and it's been a long day. I know you're all probably ready to turn in."

Ben gave her a conciliatory nod. "Of course we can eat. You've gone to a great deal of trouble for us. Zach, Rob, she's not going to serve you or clean up this kitchen," he said. "Zoe, we appreciate this feast. Everyone, dig in."

The noise level resumed and as soon as everyone had what they needed, Zoe dashed off to the bathroom. She hadn't been alone all day. Sitting on the side of the tub, she put her face in her hands and let her body relax for a minute.

Ben's family took some getting used to. They argued differently than the women in her family who were brutal. The Hoods were honest, but they weren't out to do permanent damage.

She pulled the band from her hair, feeling some of the tension leave her body through her shoulders. A peaceful night's sleep would be welcome. Despite everything, it felt good not having to captain her own ship for once in her life. She was in charge, but Ben was technically more in charge, and he was being responsible. She liked him in the so-called ghost position. He was working, but his job was to look after her.

There was something liberating about relinquishing control of everything—if only for a little while—to a man who knew how to handle responsibility without being abusive.

Sighing, Zoe rubbed her eyes and absorbed the sounds of the night and the environment around her. The Hoods had proven themselves to be decent people, so she couldn't understand why she felt herself holding back her feelings for Ben.

She'd enjoyed making out with and making love to him. He'd made sure she was satisfied, but even more than that there was a caring gene in him that didn't go unnoticed. She'd seen it in his reaction to her, but also in how he treated Loren.

But maybe he was good at rescuing damsels in distress. And maybe once this case was over, the white-eyelet bed would be for someone else.

She had to keep him at a distance. Or his come-get-into-my-bed energy would wear her down and she'd be butt-naked, spread-eagle, on the king-size, pillow top.

Resting her face on her hands, Zoe let her mind wander around the subject and could hear the boisterous laughter from the kitchen. They were obviously having a good time.

She was tired, and they were still energized. How did women put up with them? They had to be animals in bed. She'd been with Ben and he'd made love to her until she'd had to run away, it had been that good. Remembering almost made her call him down the hall for a second round.

Rising, she wet her hands and rubbed them through her hair before starting a loose braid.

"Zoe, you okay in there?"

"Yes. Come in. I'm just finishing up."

Ben walked in. "You're determined to control your hair. Leave it alone. It's pretty like it is."

"It's a squirrel's tail. I need another band," she said, unable to find the one she'd had before.

Seeing it on the floor, she picked it up and snapped it around the ends, when Ben caught her around the waist.

"Just what do you think you're doing?" she whispered.

"Collecting on a portion of my debt." He leaned against the sink and brought her against him.

"That's unfair, Ben." She lost her grip on her hair and the band spiraled off, falling onto the floor again. "You made the rule of no fooling around while we're working together."

"I love that you have such a good memory. But if you remember correctly, our business concluded with the arrest of your sister. We declared the case closed."

He urged her leg on top of his and she held herself back. He was right. He stroked the inseam of her left leg and buried his nose in her neck, planting light kisses under her jaw. "You smell delicious. Like lavender and something else."

"That's chicken," she said, wanting to wrap her arms around him. "So how are we working together now?"

"Pro bono."

"I see." She was surprised to find herself straining to feel more pressure from his fingers. "So that means the old rule is out?"

"It can be. What do you want?"

"You, but—"

"Tell me why. Tell me what happened before."

Zoe tried to pull away. The intimacy was too much. She didn't want to expose her insecurities and the judgments she'd made about all men. "I don't want to talk about this."

"You never want to talk about it, but you feel better after you do. Fine, as long as you're here, you won't sleep away from me. I want you, do you understand?"

She nodded, rocking back and forth.

"Now let's go eat and get rid of your company."

"They're your relatives."

He lifted her shirt and kissed her bruised ribs. "But you invited them and that's the only reason those greedy men are here. If it was up to me, I'd have you on the floor or in the bed naked right now."

Zoe could hardly contain her desire. "Let's hurry them the hell up."

Ben breathed hard and pulled her shirt down. "Go ahead," he told her. "I need a couple minutes."

"I can wait for you," she offered.

"Zoe, if you stay, we won't get there."

Her phone vibrated and she answered. "Hello? Yes, this is Zoe McKnight. Hi, Mr. Turner. Good to hear from you."

Ben got close enough to listen to the conversation. "Move up our meeting?"

"Yes, Zoe. I'm going to be in Atlanta this week and I wanted to get together. unfortunately next week won't be good for me. I have tomorrow available at one o'clock."

"That's such short notice. Tomorrow, I don't know."

Ben nodded.

"I'm a busy man and this is my one opportunity to see you. Are you interested in the real estate or not?"

"I am, Mr. Turner."

"Can you meet at my office in the Duluth area?"

"That's fine," Zoe said. "Good night. Ben, I'm in trouble. I'm not ready."

Chapter 15

The dishwasher had been turned on and the floor swept, and Ben turned off the kitchen lights. The house was quiet, but he knew Rob was still upstairs in his office working.

Ben couldn't wait to get to Zoe and lay her fears to rest. She'd be fine with Turner tomorrow. She was as prepared as she could be when dealing with an unknown entity.

Ben still had five other cases to review with Rob that were active, but Zoe's took priority over them all. It was rare when the entire Hood team was on one case, but hers was moving quickly.

He took the stairs, the moonlight shining through the arched foyer glass. Hugh had stopped by but he and Zach had left thirty minutes ago, taking a plate of leftovers, and Ben was glad to send them home. They were all bachelors, and home-cooked food was hard to come by these days. Besides, Zoe seemed happy to be with his family, asking lots of questions and joking with the guys. Now all Ben could think of was her.

Heading down the hall to the office he shared when Rob was over, Ben walked in and saw the image on the computer screen and stopped in the doorway. DeLinda, Rob's deceased wife, blew kisses and waved.

Rob had watched this video a thousand times after she died, and Ben knew it was seeing Loren that had triggered this sudden trip of nostalgia. The women favored, granted, but Rob would be a fool to try to get with someone like Loren who was so wounded. She'd suffered a great trauma, and Rob needed a woman that was whole.

Seeing Loren today had probably opened an old wound.

DeLinda was waving on the screen again, saying good-bye just before she boarded a plane to Ohio to see her ailing mother. She'd gone to the pharmacy one night for some antinausea medicine and had gotten kidnapped, raped and killed.

"Hey, anything interesting going on?" Ben sat at his desk, watching DeLinda, too. She'd been one of the nicest people he'd ever met.

Rob tapped a key on the computer and her image disappeared. "No, I'm tripping. Tired, I guess. Loren looks a lot like her, her complexion is lighter, though. Seeing her tonight was shocking." Rob scrubbed his face with his hands. He was tired and he looked lonely. Ben felt pain for his twin.

"Don't confuse the two women, Rob. Loren is damaged goods. We don't know what happened, but it's bad. She couldn't look any of us in the eye."

"I won't confuse anything, but if you haven't noticed, I'm pretty much a jigsaw puzzle, too." Rob closed his laptop and slid it into its bag.

The brothers faced each other.

"What are your intentions with Zoe?" Rob asked him. He took charge like any good CEO.

"Are you her father?"

"You know better than to mix Hood business and personal business, so what are you doing?"

"Protecting a friend," Ben answered.

"And she's not more than that to you?"

"No."

"You don't want more than that with Zoe, Ben?"

"I didn't say that."

"I'm warning you to be careful. The first slip up could have happened to anyone. You closed her case without really investigating all other possibilities. You've never been sloppy."

"I've already admitted to making that mistake, Rob."

"I'm saying, Ben, in any other case, that wouldn't have happened. The fact that you didn't immediately pursue Zoe tells me it could have been an innocent mistake, but you don't make mistakes, Ben." Rob got up and walked to the door. "Don't start making them now. I'm going home. Talk to you tomorrow."

"Good night." Ben stayed at his desk until he heard the beeping of the alarm being set by his brother.

Rob was wrong. Mistakes happened to everyone, but pursuing a woman he hadn't been able to get off his mind wasn't a mistake.

But out of respect for his brother and the business, he'd heed the warning. He'd hold back on making a personal move on Zoe as long as he could.

Cutting off the lights, he closed the door to the office and listened to the sounds of the house. He knew every curve, every bump and step, the smooth finish of paint and the stippled texture of the ceiling as if he were a blind man.

He liked being in the dark because it enhanced his other senses. He had only to close his eyes and he could feel the presence of another person before he saw or smelled them.

He stood at the top of the half-rounded staircase and felt Zoe's presence before he saw her. "The alarm is on."

She froze. "I need a robe."

Her voice was shaking, but she wasn't defiant. Still, she didn't turn around or raise her voice. She was going to leave with or without him. "Do you want the code?"

"Just like that?"

Ben walked down the stairs. She didn't even have on shoes.

"Where are you going barefoot?"

Her keys rattled as she scratched her brow with the car key. She looked at her feet and then at him. He saw her tired eyes in the moonlight. "To the store to get some conditioner and some flip-flops."

He pulled her close and her mass of hair tickled his face. "You want to go home," he told her.

She nodded.

"Come on."

They left the house and climbed into his car.

Before Ben pulled onto the interstate, Zoe settled in her seat and he thought she was asleep.

"Don't you ever sleep?" she asked.

"Not when I'm on the job."

"When we were first together, you didn't sleep then, either."

He laughed. "I was trying to impress you."

She giggled and closed her eyes. "That is impressive. Men don't do that anymore."

They passed a large retail store open twenty-four hours. "You want to stop?"

Zoe shook her head. "No, I've got everything at home. Thanks."

"You're welcome. You're getting me in trouble with the rest of the team. I've already been chastised."

"I see. I'm sure you don't let clients stay at your house every day."

"You're the first."

"Then I really feel special."

"You are. Anyway, let's get in and out. I want you to have maximum coverage. I won't expose you to unnecessary danger."

"Why do you do this, Ben? It's dangerous work. There's always the threat hanging over your head that you could be hurt or killed."

"True, but there's also the threat that I could be bored to death at a desk working for someone else for the rest of my life. That would kill me."

"But aren't you afraid?"

"No."

She looked as if she didn't believe him. "You're not scared that you're going to get shot or stabbed?"

"No. If I walked through life thinking like that I'd never leave my house. You wouldn't ask that of a pilot, or a train conductor, or a bus driver or an attorney, would you?"

They gathered speed when the light turned green and he made a right off Mountain Industrial in Clarkston onto her sleeping street. "No, I guess not. But what happens when you can't do this anymore?"

"The same thing that happens to everyone else. I do something else or retire."

"What are your goals, Ben?"

"To be independently wealthy. Yours?"

Zoe looked at her house. "The same as yours."

He slowed the car to a crawl. "Everything look okay?"

"Yes. That looks like my father's car." Zoe craned her neck to see. "It is Daddy. What's he doing over here?"

"I don't know. Call his cell."

Zoe dialed and her father picked up on the first ring. "Dad, what are you doing outside my house?"

"Keeping an eye on things. It's all quiet. That you that just passed me?"

"Yes, it's Ben and me. You want to come in? That can't be good for your hip."

"This beats sitting in the house all day. Me and Fred are fine, but we're going home, hot dog. It's midnight."

"Thanks, Daddy."

"Tell Ben I said good night."

"I will."

Zoe watched her father pull off before Ben pulled onto her driveway. "My dad is the coolest guy. I guess he was more worried about me than he let on."

Ben chuckled at her and got out the car.

"What," she asked, as they walked up the walkway to the front door, wet leaves tumbling underfoot from the automatic sprinkler system.

"You think your father is cool. That's cool." He put his arm around her shoulder and kissed her temple. "Girl, I love your hair."

"I look like a younger version of Diana Ross."

"Have you seen her pictures from the seventies? I used to have a mad crush on her."

"Now I know you're weird." Zoe opened the door and inhaled before stepping inside.

"What are you doing?" he said.

"You know how you knew I was up? You didn't see me, did you?"

"No, I felt your presence."

He walked in behind her quietly, closed and locked the door.

"I do the same, except I feel someone's presence and I can smell them." She turned into him. "You smell like verbena, pineapple and melon."

"You saying I smell like a fruit basket?"

He'd tried to back her against the wall, but she made it to the stairs before he caught her and grabbed her, sticking his finger in the waist of her pants.

Zoe giggled. "Those are some of the ingredients. There's also lavender and violet."

He grabbed her foot and ran his finger from the heel to her toes, causing her to burst into a fit of giggles.

"So I wipe flowers and fruit on my neck, is that it? I'm a sissy? Is that what you're saying?"

"No. Stop, Ben. I swear something bad will happen if you don't stop tickling my foot."

He let her foot go. "I don't even want to know."

Zoe pushed up off the stairs. "I forgot how tired I am." She looked over her shoulder at him. "You shouldn't be so sensitive. At least know what you're wearing before you attack innocent women."

"Innocent women should think before they accuse men of wearing fruit and flowers."

Zoe strolled to her room and pushed open the doors.

Ben searched for the light and found the lamp on the night stand. He turned it on thinking she'd go for her closet or bathroom, but Zoe made a bee-line for her bed. She sat down and fell back, and her hair fanned out like in a shampoo commercial.

One hand went over her head and the other rested on her stomach.

"Whoa, what are you doing?"

"Please, Ben? Just five minutes to wallow on my lovely bed. I love this thing. It's so comfortable and I missed it. Just five minutes. I know we have to go. I'm going to get up. I promise."

"Three minutes. I'll get your robe. What color is it?" He opened the doors to the closet and stepped back. "This is the biggest closet I've ever seen. Damn! It's another room."

"Quit exaggerating. It's fuchsia. First row on the right, third hanger."

"How do you know that?"

"That's where it belongs. I guess I'd better get some pajamas, too. There should be some next to the robe."

"For someone who doesn't wear pajamas, you have a lot of them."

"How do you know that?" She turned to look at him.

"You confessed it to me our first night together at the party then again right after your concussion. You said they get tangled up in the bed and make you frustrated. You prefer to go commando."

Zoe was mortified. "I talk too much when I drink cosmopolitans. No more of those for me."

"I still like your ideology on no pajamas better."

"You're a man, you would."

"Are there any you like?" he asked, feeling the silk, satins, and flimsy materials that she casually referred to as pajamas. He knew they were lingerie, but this stuff was nothing short of expensive gauze. "Damn, it's hard to believe you don't have a man with all this."

"I don't wear it to the clubs. That would make me a hooker. Please, can we stay here?"

"No, and your preference, going once, twice—"

"I don't have one."

Big mistake, Ben said to himself. He chose everything he'd ever imagined seeing on a woman and stuffed it all into a bag she had hanging on an elaborate machine full of purses and belts.

"I'll double all your bets, Ben. I want to sleep in my bed."

"As good as that sounds, no. Come on."

"You want me living at your house. Cooking and cleaning. Naked, hair all over the place. Sex machine." She yawned and curled up, tossing the lavender-and-beige chenille afghan over her feet, using one arm as her pillow and the other draped over the footboard.

Ben had to stop for a moment. She was tired and she'd been really good at doing everything he'd asked. He put the bag down at the foot of her bed and touched her leg.

"Ben, just five minutes," she said, her eyes closed, and that's when he saw that her face was wet.

He climbed on the bed behind her. "Why are you crying?"

"Not," she said softly. "Body is just downloading. Come here."

Ben got really close. She took his arm and brought it around her waist, bringing him so close he could nuzzle her neck. This was dangerous territory.

She interlocked their fingers. "Lie down with me for just an hour."

"Woman," he groaned.

She finally looked at him and her eyes pleaded for him to understand. To trust her. To listen.

She knew the second he changed his mind because she kissed him with a tenderness that made his heart skip a beat, and then another.

The pressure of her lips awoke in him a sensitivity at a depth to which he'd never known. He wanted to hold and protect her and make love to her. He could no more tear off her clothes and take her in haste than he could run over a helpless animal.

Ben pulled pillows from the top of the bed and brought the comforter with him. He set his watch for one hour and cut off the light while Zoe burrowed into her pillow.

His hands were gentle when he turned her over and spooned her. She brought their linked fingers around her waist again, and fell asleep right away.

Ben lay there in a state of semiconsciousness, aware of the rain as it moved between the leaves of the old trees and hit the ground, the aroma of fresh shampoo from her silky curls, and the responsibility he'd undertaken for the woman in his arms.

As the first hour shifted into the second and her sleep deepened, he became aware that there were few places he'd rather be. He also knew he was in big trouble because this would be the biggest secret he'd ever keep from his older brother.

Chapter 16

Zoe felt the rumble of Ben's even breathing on her back when she awakened. In her sleep she'd turned and was now flat on her stomach, and Ben was bracing her back with his hands, using her as his pillow.

She'd had a dog when she was little, Dodger McKnight, and he'd snored so loud he sounded like a train caboose. Ben wasn't as loud as Dodger, but his breathing as he slept made her feel like her old friend was back, like she was safe and nothing could harm her.

Slowly, she turned and Ben awoke instantly.

"Hey," she said, running her hand over his back to let him know everything was okay. "It's time to get up. It'll be dawn soon. We've got to get back."

Ben brought his arm up, tapping it to see his watch. "Damn it, woman, it's five o'clock."

"I know. Let's go." She nudged him, but got nowhere.

Sitting up, Zoe scooted off the bed. "You can use my bathroom. I'll use the guest bath."

Hurrying, she hit the commode first, then washed her face and brushed her teeth, and had changed clothes when Ben finished.

"We're going to bed when we get home." He took her hand.

"No, we're not. The day has already started. Besides, we need to buy groceries. Your pantry is bare."

"I'll concede on that one, but, baby, I'm tired. We only slept three hours."

"I slept well." Zoe was at the top of the stairs when she stopped. "Did you hear that?" she whispered.

"What?"

She was suddenly behind Ben and he was blocking her.

They both listened to the silence for several minutes. "I guess it's just the house settling," she said.

"We're both paranoid because I thought I heard something, too. Get your computer and let's go. I have your other stuff."

Zoe went back for the bag, amazed that she'd forgotten her computer, the one thing she'd wanted so badly. Good thing he'd reminded her. She stabbed her feet into her sandals, hurried down the stairs behind Ben and walked out the door.

Back at Ben's house, Ben flipped pancakes as Zoe sat at the breakfast table, earpiece in as she typed messages into her calendar on the computer. She loved that his kitchen faced the yard so that one could commune with nature over their morning coffee, whereas at her house if she opened the blinds, she got to wave at the neighbors who weren't always fond of wearing robes.

Zoe drank her coffee and listened to voice mail. "Zoe,

it's Ireland. I want to talk to you about a promotion to district manager. Face it, you need one. I've been here a while, and I believe I've proven myself to be a loyal store manager. We're about to expand and you need someone on your team that knows how this company is run. I'm that person. Please call so we can discuss in detail. I look forward to talking to you, goodbye."

Zoe closed her eyes and tapped her pen on her forehead. Ireland was right, but she'd thought of not hiring for that position for a few more months. Then again, she didn't want to lose a valued employee. Zoe sighed and pursed her lips.

She pressed the button to leave a message for Ireland. "Ireland, it's Zoe. You're right. I do need a second in command. You are incredibly valuable to the Zoe's Diamonds family and have proven that your knowledge and experience are worthy assets to the company. I'd like to offer you a promotion not as a district manager but as a regional manager. That position will cover all four stores. I appreciate your honesty and look forward to a bright future together. I will forward you all resumes that I have received so that we may begin the hiring process for the new stores. I'll call you soon. Bye."

"Hi, Zoe, this is Holly and William from St. Thomas. We've got some new designs for ya to see. We can't wait for ya ta get down here on the fourteenth. The room isn't ready because of the storm, but we've got the bungalow for ya. Send us some more of your sketches. William is worried since we haven't heard from ya, girl, but I told him ya busy. Take care, girl. Lata."

Holly's lovely accent seeped under her skin, and Zoe took a big breath and could already feel herself relaxing even though this wouldn't be a vacation.

She loved going to see her friends and favorite jewelry

makers, but it was also the island of St. Thomas that inspired her. Not the shopping district where the tourists crowded the streets, but the markets where natives shopped. Everything was fresh, and people knew Holly and William and respected them.

Zoe loved going to their home in the hills where the wind danced with the curtains, and lush aromas wafted from the kitchen. William would work in their sweltering workshop until all hours of the night while she and Holly talked design and materials. They'd go on scavenger hunts to see what types of metals and raw materials they could find in junk yards, and would end up in the workshop, too, sifting through the cases she'd brought from the States, and then the designing would begin.

Though each of them had their own specialty, their ideas overlapped, and often blended until they'd made something so far superior from where it started, even they were impressed.

Holly and William had been married for twenty years and their timeless romance seeped into each piece.

Zoe pulled up the designs she'd sent to Holly and William for their opinions and the thrill she'd felt two years ago when she'd delivered the pictures still coursed through her. They'd come so far from being street vendors.

Ben walked over and Zoe downsized the screen.

"What you hiding?" he asked, heading back to the stove.

"Nothing. I'm trying to work here," she snapped.

"You yelled at me," he said so casually he may as well have been asking for a pair of socks. "So I'm exercising my bet for a kiss option. Turkey bacon or regular?"

He ate a piece and held up the two different types for her to choose.

Zoe didn't know what to say, waiting for the explosion

of anger that would result in an argument. He wanted to combat anger with affection? Didn't he know how to fight?

Ben was such a strange man. He was trying to get closer to her, but wasn't pressing her for details, berating or condemning her. Now she felt silly for being so paranoid. He wasn't Charles and he wasn't trying to steal her business.

"Regular, please," she said, unsure if she was supposed to say something else mean or not.

He cut off the stove and filled her plate with bacon, grits and eggs, and poured orange juice into a champagne flute. "Come here," he said.

Was he going to yell in her face? Ben really didn't seem the type. She stayed seated and acted as if she hadn't heard him.

"Zoe, come here."

She finally walked over, keeping her gaze on the jogging suit he'd changed into once they'd gotten back to his house. "What?"

"What's wrong with you?"

Ben looked down at her and she felt like a chastised child. "I'm stressing. I've got the meeting this afternoon and I've got to be ready. My jewelry designers are expecting me in St. Thomas on the fourteenth. I hate that I've done nothing to Gordo. He bought jewelry from someone who stole it and I feel as if I let him walk away scot-free. I don't know what's happening between you and me. I snapped at you and I should have apologized, but then I thought you were starting a fight and you weren't, and then I didn't know what to do. I was hiding my jewelry designs that I've never shared with anyone except my designers."

"First things first. We're going to handle your meeting with Mitchell Turner. You won't be going alone, so stop stressing over that. Second, I love St. Thomas, so I'll go with you and you'll be protected the entire time. Third, Gordo isn't walking away scot-free. He's helping us find the fake Zoe McKnight."

"Why didn't I know this?"

"Because you were healing, and we've been moving quickly on the details of everything. Hugh got some good information on Turner that you and I need to review before the meeting."

"What kind of information?"

"Regarding how he cheated past owners and took their money before running them out of business."

Zoe sighed heavily. "Is everything so sinister with you?" Her shoulders slumped and she gazed out the window.

"I'm not trying to hurt you," he said.

"Is Gordo tied to Turner?"

Ben shook his head. "He, unfortunately, bought a hot necklace."

"Okay," she whispered. "Let him keep it with my best wishes. I just want to know who's trying to hurt me the worst. If it's not him, then who? I've lost a sister, my family is divided over this and I'm lost. I look at how close your family is and I can't help but want the same thing."

Sorrow flashed in his eyes momentarily.

"You realize I want that for you, too."

"I know." His sincerity brought them closer. Zoe pulled her fingers through her straight hair, glad that she'd been able to spend an hour fixing it once they'd gotten back to Ben's house.

"What else?" he asked.

"I was going to apologize to you," she said, and sucked her lips into her mouth. This time she did look at Ben and his gaze became quizzical.

"And you can't?"

"I can. I shouldn't have snapped at you," she managed softly.

"Why are you afraid to apologize?" he asked, standing beside her.

"I was always told *I'm sorry* doesn't fix anything. That it's a useless statement. I guess my father felt that in his line of work people made permanent mistakes. The phrase couldn't reverse anything. I'm not a child and I know better. I should be better at apologizing."

"It fixes a lot of things," Ben told her. "Try it."

Zoe fidgeted with the belt of her sweat suit. "I'm sorry." She started away and Ben caught her wrist.

"Come here. Come here. It doesn't have to hurt."

"What?" She was frustrated now, not wanting to do any more self-reflection.

"You're forgiven," he said against her temple. "Okay?"

She nodded and tried to pull away.

"The sky didn't fall in. Nobody is going to stab you. Just stand here for a minute and let the feeling pass. It's over. Never to talk about again."

"You won't throw it up in my face?"

"No. We'll fight again. People do, but we won't talk about this incident again."

Her arms were up, her fingers by her jaw, even though Ben was still holding her.

"You know what would make this all better?"

"What?"

He didn't say anything because she knew. He needed to know she accepted his forgiveness. She finally put her arms around him and the feeling slipped away.

How many petty arguments could have been settled, right or wrong, if she'd just said *I'm sorry?* Maybe things wouldn't have been so bad between her and her sister, but

Zoe let the thought fizzle as it formed. The issues couldn't be fixed with a simple phrase.

She raised up on her toes and kissed him. All she knew was that what she had with Ben made her *feel* safe. He made *I'm sorry* feel like it should—a genuine apology, words meant to erase a wrong.

He could quickly overpower her, but that wasn't his goal. He was a powerful man, allowing her to be who she was—a sexy, seductive woman.

Zoe felt as if something in her had been unleashed. He bent to her open mouth and she seduced his tongue with hers, their mouths fighting to become closer.

When a groan tore from his throat, she kissed up his jaw to his ear and tugged on the lobe with her teeth before whispering, "I want you right now."

Zoe had her hands beneath his shirt and ran her nails down his back and into his pants, over his bottom. The result was an amazing body shiver that resembled a climax.

"You're in big trouble," he said.

Zoe took Ben's hand and guided him up the stairs. "I like your kind of trouble."

In the bedroom, Zoe kicked off her shoes and when he took her to his bed, she stood on it, and helped him off with his jacket and then his shirt.

Her top and pants were next. "Are you always braless?"

"Always after work," she said, as she kissed up his side and ended at his nipple. His fingers got lost in her hair. "And on my days off," she told him as she planted kisses in the center of his chest, and trailed her tongue up to his mouth and sucked his bottom lip. She stripped off his pants in seconds and his member bobbed against her lips. Zoe sucked him in, his hands controlling the flow, her hands and nails creating sensations that had him in a constant state of pleasure.

"Damn girl, you're going to kill me."

"I hope not. Ben, I don't wear underwear on the weekend."

Zoe went airborne and she squealed when she hit the mattress on her back with him on top of her.

"You're a seductress, is that it?"

"Yes." She rolled on top of him, her hair in his face. He seemed to love it. "Condom?" she asked.

He reached into the bedside drawer and pulled out a few. Zoe rolled it on and stretched her long legs until she was in his lap. There she took her time, their bodies still separate, enjoying the sensations of his open mouth on her back and shoulders, her sensitive nipples and palms. His lips, and the heat of his breath on the bend in her arms, and behind her knees, her neck and wrists made her want to be closer to him, made her want to give all of herself to him.

He claimed her with his mouth and she climaxed in a slow arc that lifted her back off the bed. What she wanted was him inside of her, to feel the weight of him on her body, the heat of his skin, the pressure of his sex in hers. She'd given him just about everything else. Now she was giving him her.

Zoe brought her hands up his back to his neck and called his name and he stretched above her. They both looked down as he guided himself into her and she gripped him, holding with her arms and legs and sex.

He cupped her bottom and drove himself into her, and Zoe gasped, feeling him deeper, wanting more. She opened and pushed against him, letting him know she would take all he had.

"More?" he asked.

"More," she told him, and he let go, making love to her as passionately as he approached life.

His hands were everywhere. His mouth and tongue, too,

and when he finally had her the last time, Zoe knew she could want no other man after him.

Ben awoke and watched Zoe sleep. She lay partially on her stomach, her arms beneath her. She'd been right when she said her hair was everywhere. In her sleep, she was so innocent and lovely. Awake, lively and loveable. He loved all versions of her.

Her eyes opened. "I'm resting. Stop trying to seduce me," she said in a sexy voice. "I'm not a sex machine."

"Are you sure about that?" He drew his thumb down her back.

"You know how I hate when you do that," she said with a smile.

His brow shot up as he moved her hair to bite her shoulder while drawing his thumb closer to her bottom. "You hate this? Are you positive?"

Zoe opened her legs wider, a smile on her face. "Yes, you dirty man. You're constantly doing things to me that drive me crazy like stimulating me with your fingers."

Her gasp enticed him nearly as much as her wet folds.

Ben kissed Zoe's ear. "How do you feel, darling?"

"Better than ever before." Zoe opened wider and Ben bent and kissed her bottom, making her laugh. From her feet to the top of her thighs he ran his tongue and lips until her moans became cries of pleasure.

"More, Zoe?" he asked, moving on top of her back. She bent her knees.

"Yes," she said. "Yes."

Ben entered her from behind, determined to make this lovemaking her most pleasurable. He slowed down, moving in and out of her slowly to heighten the sensuality, but she turned and flipped that black mane of hair to the side.

She reached back and grabbed his thigh. "More, baby. More now."

How could he resist a request so eloquent? Ben bent down and stretched to kiss her mouth before grabbing her hips and pushing into her with force. Her back arched and she cried out. Their bodies synched and he spread her knees a bit wider wanting her to know that the beauty in making love to him was that it would never be the same.

"Ben," she cried.

"Come, baby."

Seconds later she cried out again and her body tensed in a beautiful climax. Ben held Zoe, surprised that she tightened so much. He felt as if a vacuum had closed over his manhood. She released and opened again, pulling him tighter, his own release came in a powerful wave.

Ben lay on Zoe's back, their bodies still joined.

"That was amazing," she said.

He couldn't find the right words.

Zoe wiggled and moved until he rolled over. "I'd better get ready. We have a long day ahead of us."

Ben silently berated himself as he watched her hurry away. He wanted to stop time and just hold her, but soon life would return to normal. And that meant life without Zoe. He knew he'd have to get used to that again.

Chapter 17

To Zoe, Mitchell Turner was a weasel, but his office was suited for a king. He kept them waiting for ninety minutes and now that they were in his inner sanctum, he had the nerve to take a phone call.

Zoe and Ben sat at his desk, and no matter how much Zoe tried to stifle her nervousness, she couldn't help but feel as if she were facing her elementary school principal.

Except she was almost positive Principal Johnson had never sat in a ten-thousand-dollar office chair from Hong Kong. She didn't like Mitchell Turner. Not after all she'd learned in her debriefing meeting today. He never stopped smiling with his oversized capped teeth. Not while he read her financials, or while reading a report he pulled from a folder on the side of his desk.

Ben put his hand on her knee and quieted the nervous jumping. He made the move seem like a caress, or at least it seemed to be interpreted that way by Turner, whose smile took on a hard edge.

Zoe played along with her seductive smile to Ben.

She finally captured Turner's attention. "Question?" she asked.

"Seems your boyfriend can't wait to get you alone."

"He's not my boyfriend, he's a partner in Zoe's Diamonds, Mr. Turner. I've already explained that."

"I'm here to make sure she doesn't do any bad business."

The air was thick with testosterone and unfired gunpowder.

"I don't do business with silent partners. You may be excused, Mr. Hood. These talks are confidential."

"Come on, Zoe. Mr. Turner doesn't want to do business with us." Ben stood, buttoning his jacket.

Zoe rose to leave.

"Oh, I want to continue doing business with Ms. McKnight."

"Then why not speak to me and my partner, Mr. Turner? You mentioned you were only here for a short time. My stores will bring in a projected average of ten million dollars of revenue to your malls per year over the next three years. Is that something you want to walk away from? I've never made a late lease payment, and I've met all the requirements you've set forth. I'm not sure why you'd want to disrupt such a lucrative relationship."

"Those numbers are lofty at best given theft or shrinkage numbers. You can't seem to control them. They seem to be climbing every month."

"I can understand your concern. I'm very concerned about the assault that happened to me, Mr. Turner, at your Peachtree Mall. I even considered pressing charges due to lax security. I have taped proof of your back-lot guard asleep on the job."

"I've heard of no such thing," Turner said, enraged. "Your attack has nothing to do with me. Was it reported?"

"Yes, Mr. Turner, to my personal investigators. They are looking into this matter and will get to the bottom of what's going on. And whoever is behind it will be brought to justice." Zoe smiled.

"I saw no such report," he retorted. "Had I seen it, we would be discussing an increase in the down payment for your two additional stores."

Ben put his hand on Turner's desk. "You are not suggesting we punish a female victim, are you? That would smack of discrimination, and, as an attorney, I can assure you women's rights organizations and the media would eat you alive. Your malls would suffer with females being your prominent shopping demographic."

"But," Zoe said in a breathy voice, retaking her seat. "I decided against such action because of our future lucrative business together."

Turner's mouth hung open in surprise. "I was able to defend myself against the attacker, so I considered it an isolated incident. Has an attack happened to any other jeweler, Mr. Turner?"

"No, Ms. McKnight. Now—"

"I'd want to know because if there was ever any violence again, I'd pull my money, my business and walk away. My life is far more important than a few gems. I cut you off a moment ago. You were going to talk about safety for your tenants, right?"

"No, I wasn't. I was going to talk about your theft numbers."

"Fine, back to that. What's your question?"

"They're high. I'm afraid—"

"I'm glad you mentioned how high they are, because that's a concern of ours, too. Right, Ben?"

"That's right."

"But they're not nearly as high as Anthony and Vera Tatum's. Nineteen percent." Ben gave her a wave of the hand to go on. "Harry and Francis Montgomery's jewelry store, twenty-two percent. I can certainly see why they went out of business in a year."

"Those records are confidential."

"I was able to obtain them from the public bankruptcy records," Zoe explained innocently.

"None of this excuses the fact that your numbers are high, and because of that, your deposits are going to increase substantially."

Zoe looked at Ben. "I was afraid he was going to say that. I was afraid you were going to say I was at fault for my store getting broken into repeatedly when I have a notarized statement from your security guard that he lost his store keys."

He looked incredulous, his face bright red. "What in the hell does that have to do with me? You haven't allowed anyone to have keys to your store, Ms. McKnight?"

"That's right, I haven't. Not the front of my store. I had those locks changed and never got around to having more keys made. But your guard's keys, they're to the back door which leads right into my stockroom. That allows full access to my store and that's where I was brutally attacked." She pulled a makeup wipe from her bag and rubbed the bottom of her chin showing the bruise.

"I was viciously attacked leaving my store by someone who had a key, Mr. Turner. Your guard admitted to my security agent that he was asleep on the job. He confessed to doing no patrols. Therefore, you're liable."

"Do you have statement to that fact?"

"He signed a statement and it is notarized."

"Who is this man?" Turner asked, looking dangerous, pen in hand.

"He's chosen to remain anonymous."

"You could have made this up."

Mitchell Turner watched the DVD player she'd sat on the desk showing the fight between her and the perpetrator.

"Ben, the photos, please?"

Ben reached inside his jacket pocket, but Turner held up his hand, his face sick-looking at the point where she broke the man's nose. "That's not necessary."

"I'm glad you said that. Thankfully, Zoe had her gun." Ben had made a steeple with his hands and sat up straight in his chair. "And she knows how to use it."

Turner wasn't smiling anymore. The look in his eyes said he wanted both of them dead and gone.

"You had a gun on my premises? That's a violation of all kinds of codes," he said, but couldn't name any.

"Don't worry." Zoe put her permit on his desk and he pushed back in his expensive chair not wanting to look at it. "I'm licensed to carry a concealed weapon."

"That's good to know," Turner said without the rancor she believed he intended.

"Why would you want to know that?" Ben asked him, looking innocently quizzical.

"Well, I—I wouldn't want you to hurt yourself or someone needlessly."

"The way you feel about your wife and daughter is the way I feel about Zoe. Think of how badly you'd hurt a man for hurting your baby girl. How old is she?"

"Madison is seven."

Ben didn't blink. "I believe in the principle of tens. One

of Zoe's hands gets hurt, a man pays with his fingers and toes. Both of her hands, then his fingers and toes, and any other loose appendage and organs until I get to a hundred. You see how quickly that could be painful for someone?"

Turner's eyes narrowed. "What was your name again?"

"Ben," Zoe chastised. "Stop it. Now you've changed the subject. Mr. Turner, I've got to be on my way in a few moments. I'll conclude by saying it's not fair for you to ask me to pay a higher deposit when your security is clearly negligent. If thieves see there's enforcement, they'll take their crimes elsewhere."

"Ms. McKnight, I'm glad to see you're on the mend, but the attack on you has nothing to do with me. If men want to come into your store and steal necklaces, how is that my fault? I have to protect my investment and the interest of all the tenants."

"I understand, but I know you're a smart businessman. The attack on a female when security was lax won't bode well for you in the media. And a lawsuit will bring bad publicity. We'll stay with the original percentage rates and deposits, and I'll be happy to do business with you."

Turner's smile remained, but it never reached his eyes. "I'll think about it."

"I've consulted with my attorney here, and we're available to sign the final contracts a week from Monday."

"Why so long?" he asked, suddenly suspicious.

"I've got unfinished business—" Zoe said.

"Zoe, now we don't want to tell everything," Ben said in a confidential tone.

Zoe gave Ben a flirtatious smile. "You're right. A week from Monday." She reached across the desk, leaving Turner no choice but to stand and shake her hand.

"Mr. Turner, what a strong grip." Zoe increased hers in degrees until he stopped squeezing. "It's been a pleasure."

He never spoke.

"He's more guilty than Faye, that's for sure, but why?"

"I don't know him. Why does he want to destroy me?"

"I wouldn't say destroy, but he wants to cripple your business and the reason is still a mystery. You definitely gave him a lot to think about. I'm impressed. Where'd you get pictures of his guard sleeping?"

"I didn't say the pictures were of his guard, did I?"

Zoe sat back in the comfort of her seat. "I wanted him to know he can't push me around. That chair he was sitting his big butt in cost ten grand. I know because I sat in one when I was decorating my office. The price tag made me keep moving."

"That's crazy. I bought mine at the office-supply store," Ben said.

Zoe nodded. "No kidding. Don't think I didn't notice that he wasn't sympathetic to me getting beat up. He didn't care about anything. All he cared about was charging me more money."

"Why do you want to do business with that snake?"

"Ben, look around you. Mitchell Turner has the best mall real estate in the business. I can't beat that. If I do business with someone else, I won't have the same traffic and my jewelry deserves the best avenue for visual traffic."

"At what cost, though?" He held her chin and kissed her lips. "You're worth too much to me to get hurt over jewelry."

"Jewelry is my life."

Ben pressed a kiss into her collarbone. "It isn't. You've made it your life to replace love. Come on. Let's get some work done so we can go to bed early."

Zoe waited for Ben to open her door, feeling lonely for the first time since she'd been with him. He'd only been out of the car for a few seconds, but his words reminded her of the hollow spaces, those months and years of loneliness that she'd hated and had forgotten since she'd been with him.

He opened her door and offered her his hand and she took it. Immediately, she pulled her hair back and he took a call.

"Good news. Zach found Cooke, the guy who installed the fake sensors. He was out on some kind of mandatory work program. He'll be back day after tomorrow and that's when we'll pay him a visit. Come on, let's go inside. I'm in the mood to buy some jewelry."

Zoe patted his hand. "Deal. Then I'm buying you something. I've got just the perfect thing."

Chapter 18

As Ben's legs remained tangled with the sheets, a soft snore rumbled from his side of the bed. Zoe tiptoed from the room to shower and flat iron her hair. She looked at herself closely in the mirror. Ben's towel engulfed her body as she stood in his bathroom, her bag on the floor, her clothes in his hamper. They were nearly living together, she'd been at his house so long. And she was quite content—except she needed more clothes.

At the end of her marriage she'd vowed not to love another man, yet Ben had worked his way into her bloodstream in a compelling way that had her smiling in the mirror as she gazed at herself. Zoe hurried to finish her hair and she wanted to be out of the way. Ben would be awake soon. The marks from the attack had faded to light bruises and didn't hurt anymore.

Ben didn't notice them as he'd loved her body this

morning. Just thinking about how he'd taken her nearly drove her back to bed, but she was a grown-up. She couldn't play all day. She showered and cleaned the bathroom a little and put the supplies away.

Her stomach growled loudly and she patted it, thinking about the last time she'd eaten. The distraction had been so much better than food. Better than the bacon they fixed every day and usually ate after making love.

She opened the door to the bathroom to let the steam out, and applied lotion before pulling on her work clothes.

"Ben?"

He was gone, and she wondered how a man his size could move so quietly. He was a big man with a healthy appetite for passionate lovemaking that matched her own. Perhaps they were meant to be together, she thought, as she made the bed, and straightened her bags before dragging them into his closet. But that was a future she couldn't visualize yet. Not with the St. Thomas trip about to occur and her stores opening soon.

Work was still her focal point. Zoe dressed for work, put on her makeup and jewelry, and headed down the stairs. A commotion in the kitchen stopped her.

"You need to be professional. Screwing a client is out of line."

"Don't say that again, Rob, I'm warning you."

"Well, what do you call it?"

"None of you damned business."

Zoe couldn't believe Ben spoke to his brother that way. Women were in the kitchen, too, and one of them told Ben and Rob to take their loudness into the other room.

"If anything happens to her it's going to be on your head. Where were you the other morning? I came by and your car was gone."

"Watching Zoe. That's all you need to know."

"That's not all. You're risking this entire operation for a piece—"

"Robinson Hood, if you say a piece of ass and your brother busts you in the lip, you'll deserve it. How did you meet your wife, DeLinda?"

Zoe's eyes widened as she tore the skin off her bottom lip with her teeth. The woman who spoke had humor in her voice, but she didn't sound as if she took too much from them, either. Zoe was curious to see her, but didn't want to walk in and embarrass anyone, least of all Ben.

"Xan, stay out of this. I'm trying to show him how to avoid heartache and get him off my path for his own good."

"Your brother is a grown-up and he can make his own mistakes without you standing in the way. Now move."

"All right, Alexandria. When he falls flat on his face—"

"We'll all be here to laugh at him," she finished, and they all cracked up.

"You're real nice," Ben said, before Zoe heard kissing. She assumed the sister was kissing them both.

"Ben's a grown man and if he wants to make mistakes with his eyes wide open, who are you to stop him? Let me tell you something else. DeLinda wasn't in Atlanta when she was killed. Some things in life are fate, no matter how terrible they are. So get out of your brother's way and let him live his life."

"Mama was wrong for always telling you to take care of your younger brother," another woman said. "You're older than him by four whole minutes."

"Amelia is right," Xan agreed. "You're taking your role too seriously. Relax, okay?"

"Okay. I'm sorry," Rob said.

"All right," Ben said.

Zoe was shocked. They'd already made up. She didn't think she and Faye would ever be the same or even better than they were from the other day.

Zoe longed to be a part of a big loving family unit like them. To be honest, she was a little hurt that her mother hadn't called to ask about her health. Sure, Zoe knew she was independent, but nothing substituted for the love and concern of her mother's voice.

"Let's move on to the meeting with Turner," Ben said. "I don't like the way he's jerking Zoe around. What did we find out about the glass?"

"It's a dead end," Zach said.

"We ride tonight." Rob sounded as if it was a done deal, but also seemed to have secrets and wasn't sharing them.

"It's like that?"

"Yeah," Rob said.

"What time?"

"Not you. You're the ghost for a reason, and if you can't do your job, you heard Zach propose to Loren. He's down."

"You want me to hit you, don't you? I'm riding tonight. Xan, you can stay with Zoe."

Zoe's Treo handheld started to ring, as did Ben's phone. Rob's started buzzing, too. Ben came into the foyer and saw Zoe. "How long have you been here?"

"A while. This is Zoe," she said into her phone. "A robbery? Where, Ireland?"

"At the Galleria store."

"Ben, what are we going to do?" Zoe asked.

"Zoe, the staff here at Peachtree is walking off the job. Debrena and Charletta quit and I'm alone."

Ben and Rob took their calls and were watching Zoe who dug flats out of her bag and traded them for the heels she'd been wearing.

"Hugh's inside the Galleria store and said it's a false alarm. It's all quiet," Rob told her.

"Ireland, where are you getting your information?"

"The manager Sophie just called and said she'd gotten jacked outside," Ireland said impatiently.

"Where, Ireland? Be specific," Zoe asked her.

"Last night, outside in the parking lot, with last night's deposit. She was too upset to stop and she thought someone was following her home, so she drove to the police station. The person drove off and she got an escort home," Zoe repeated for them to hear.

Ben came to listen to the call. "Ireland, this is Ben Hood. Did she say which station she went to?"

"No."

"I want to know why the hell I'm just hearing about this now," Zoe said into the phone.

"Zoe, I got your message and I feel a lot better about taking the promotion, but the staff hasn't seen or heard from you and they're afraid. I've done all I can. You've got to show your face or they're going to keep quitting."

Zoe shook her head, knowing Ireland was right. "I understand. I'm on my way now."

"Getting back to Sophie, I asked her why she didn't call me last night, but she gave me some BS about still not feeling well. I told her to just sit tight at her home today. You and your team were going to want to talk to her. She got a little nervous so I told her I was on my way. Zoe, just my opinion, but this stinks to high heaven."

"Why'd she call you, Ireland?"

"Because I've been around the longest. I've always told the managers if they need anything they can call me."

"Good job." Zoe felt ashamed that she hadn't thought to promote Ireland on her own.

Ben straightened with the phone. "Ireland, we've got a man inside the store. He's coming out to escort Sophie in. Do you have a last name for her?"

"Smith."

Rob caught the information and relayed it to Hugh. "Ireland, it's important that you don't approach her yourself. Wait until she's brought into the store. You'll be working with Hugh Hood. He's fully aware of who you are and he'll make sure you're in no danger. Please follow any instructions he gives you."

"Got it. Zoe?"

"Yes, Ireland?"

"We've got a situation at Peachtree. What am I going to do? You're going to need a staff for today. I'll stay in the Peachtree store, but we've got to get this worked out."

"Ireland, I'll work in Galleria all day and close. You stay in Peachtree, and if you don't mind, tomorrow we can talk about your new promotion to regional manager."

Ireland screamed. "That's awesome. I'll be glad to. Later, Boss."

Zoe ended the call and repacked her bag. "I'll need food, and Ben, I need my gun."

Zoe dumped her bag onto the floor and showed Ben her permit.

He tried to contain his smile but barely managed. "Scary. Zoe, this is the worst time for you to have a gun. You might actually use it. First things first. You need a staff and I've got one for you. Xan and Mel, come here, please."

"Who are they?"

"Our sisters."

Two tough women came to the kitchen door, and had she not been stooped down, Zoe would have taken a step back and yes ma'am'd them.

The sisters reminded her of Serena Williams. They were statuesque, muscular and confident, yet feminine.

"I'm Alexandria, known to everyone as Xan. This is Amelia, known as Mel. Honey, you look like we're scaring you to death."

"It's not that. Well, you're formidable. You two look like you could take a man apart."

"Thanks. I'm Mel." She was the shortest of the three at about five-eight.

"Girls," Rob scolded, who hurried down the stairs. "Zoe runs a very nice, feminine jewelry store. You have to look the part. Men come in there to buy jewelry for women. You can't look like you're going to skewer a man and cook him over an open pit."

"Aww, you're already ruining my day," Xan teased. "I'm going home to change. Where's the store and what time do we need to be there?"

Zoe looked at Ben. "Peachtree, and as soon as you get there would be great. Go through the food court, up the escalator, and you'll see Zoe's Diamonds. The registers aren't hard to learn. The colors we wear are black and fuchsia. But you can wear a white top if you don't have those. I'll pay you, of course."

The ladies looked surprised. "Wow, we really like you. Don't worry," Mel said. "We won't let you down."

"Doing this won't interfere with your regular jobs?" Zoe asked.

"I'm really a doctor," Xan said. "Mel's the mom of us all and owns her own company, but we make our own schedules. In fact, we're at work right now. We're on the Hood trap team. We meet husbands for wives to see if they're cheating. See you later," Mel said, and headed out the door.

Zoe's mouth hung open and Ben nudged her lip up.

Anger made her sides hurt and she pointed at Ben. "I should have been at work, and not here. I'm losing staff and not focusing. What was I thinking?"

"You can't predict everything," Ben told her. "We know who's doing this and we're working to find out why. We're riding on Cooke tonight, you know that."

"But I keep getting lulled into this false sense of security. That's called Fool's Paradise because only idiots live there."

"Zoe, they didn't get the store, they got the manager," Rob informed her. "This is entirely different and who's to say this is even related? This stinks, just like your sister's robbery was unrelated."

"I don't care. This is about me! I feel like I'm under siege. Like they're going to destroy me. I want you to get them first and maybe if I'm not here with you, we'll get them faster."

"Zoe, we're making progress. Cooke is back tomorrow and we'll get what we need then. Don't lose it now," Ben told her.

"That's exactly what I'm doing." She went over and kissed him in front of Rob and tried not to cry. Every part of her was at war. Should she stay or go? Was she thinking rationally or not? Her staff was getting robbed and quitting and she was making love and sleeping through the night.

Something definitely needed to change.

"As much as I hate to say it, Rob is right. I can't keep a clear head and be with you. This business means everything to me. If I don't have it, I don't have anything."

"Zoe, you're panicking."

"I know, Ben. That's all I know to do at this point." She released his hands. "Rob, if you insist on me having a bodyguard, it has to be you."

Chapter 19

Ben reread Mitchell Turner's credit report, then his real estate holdings, the bank statements he could get his hands on, and then the private contracts that had *fallen* into his lap with other vendors.

Four hours later, he was even more confused. He couldn't find a single reason why he'd want to sabotage Zoe or her business. On paper, Mitchell Turner was solvent and his malls were making money hand over fist. Their bills were paid on time and they had a triple-A rating with the top bureaus in the country. So why did all of the field agents get a resounding *no comment* and a hang up when they asked for personal reference on Mitchell Turner?

Not a single individual was even willing to discuss the man or their dealings with him.

Alarm bells were ringing like those for a hurricane warning.

If people were happy, they loved to talk about it, but when they weren't, they still loved to talk about it.

When Ben dragged Arthur Cooke across the kitchen counter in his mobile home and banged his head into the refrigerator, he didn't feel an ounce of sympathy for the man and his weak pleas. Besides, Cooke had hit him with a beer bottle in the shoulder and Ben hated that he was bleeding.

"I asked you a question and I don't repeat myself. Gas on in the stove?" Ben asked Zachary.

"Yeah, we're about to cook us some June goose." His laugh was without humor.

Cooke's weak attempt to get away only made Ben more resolved to make him suffer. Ben had him by the neck and stepped on his knee.

"I was hired to break in to the store and steal the jewelry. Bust the place up a little. That's all."

"Why'd you hit her?"

"It'll pop in three seconds," Zachary told Cooke, shining the flashlight in his face. "This is the fun part. You want me to call the cops?" he asked Cooke. "Is he being too rough on you? You've got all these fake IDs. Other people's mail, which means mail fraud. I'm sure you being a felon and all, the cops would want to know about this. You're probably not a total bad guy and what's happening ain't right. You beat up a woman and you're getting your ass kicked, but dude, you shoulda found Jesus in the joint and you could've saved yourself a good whooping."

His knee popped and Cooke howled. He sobbed, trying to hold his leg, while Ben still had him by the head.

Zach shone the light on Rob, who stood in the doorway

watching. He tapped his watch. "Guess he took too long to answer."

"He's fixated on her. Wants her stores and her designs. At first I thought it was business, but it seems personal with her," he sobbed. "He sold one of her necklaces, then got mad and keeps the rest in his safe in his house."

"Who is he?" Ben asked, hating that whoever it was not only wanted to destroy her business, but seemed to want to destroy Zoe personally.

Cooke continued to cry. "If I tell you who he is, I'm as good as dead."

"I'm no killer," Ben told him. The room was as black as Ben's clothes and Cooke would never be able to identify any of them. "I get revenge."

He banged Cooke's head against the cheap wooden table, the door frame and the door of the stove.

"Please, no. Please."

"Did she beg you to stop hitting her?"

"No, she never said a word. Please, believe me."

Ben popped him in the forehead. "You ever heard that a man isn't supposed to put his hands on a woman?"

"She was determined to get me. She kept hitting me back, and she got me in the nose with an uppercut. I kept hitting her when I realized she knew judo, or jujitsu, or some mess. She was hurting me. Please have mercy on me."

His words ate Ben up inside and he wanted to murder Cooke. He was so glad Rob and Zach were in this house with him or little pieces of Cooke would be all over the walls.

Ben squeezed until Cooke squealed. Revenge for Zoe felt great. This man had had no right to put his hands on her and since he had, he was paying in broken bones.

"A man begging for mercy. That's a funny thing, don't you think so?"

"I do," Zach replied. "Personally, I don't feel sorry for him. Especially after I see the ring that marked up her chest. Naw, I don't think so at all."

Ben shoved Cooke's head in the stove and let him struggle a bit before pulling him out. "Who is he?"

"You gonna kill me?"

Ben tried to shove all of Cooke in the oven.

"Turner! Mitchell Turner. He's been shaking down jewelers for years."

Ben released him and they left as silently as they had arrived.

Chapter 20

Ben's sisters were outspoken women who shared their opinions and didn't care what people thought about them.

Zoe had thought it was a recipe for disaster when they'd walked into the store talking loud, not looking like her usual associates who were always sleek and sexy. But she'd been wrong. The gates of the store had been raised at ten, and the tough women turned into sexy vixens, and they lured men and women into Zoe's like never before.

Had she not seen it with her own eyes, Zoe wouldn't have believed it. They charmed money out of customers, making the cash register hum until it smoked.

After the second hour of ten-thousand-dollar sales, Zoe called Rob to help on gift wrap and she ran the register for the next twelve straight hours.

"You guys are coming back tomorrow?" Zoe asked, late that night at Ben's kitchen table.

"Yes," Mel said, sounding as if she'd been used. Then she flashed Zoe with a smile so similar to Ben's, Zoe had to look away.

"Can I ask you ladies something?" Zoe said.

"Sure." They crowded around the breakfast table and Mel passed out beer.

"What does is mean to ride? The men said it earlier before they left."

A look passed between the sisters that said she was an outsider.

Xan looked her in the eye. "It means the men are going to handle their business. They're going to fight injustice and right a wrong."

"They went for me, didn't they?"

"We don't ask." Mel bit her thumb and pulled off a nail. "I don't ask. Xan knows because she can stomach stitching wounds. I just maintain the cars."

"You, Mel?"

"That's right. I'm the mom, and the resident grease monkey. Got a problem with that?" she asked in a quiet voice.

Zoe shrugged. "No, everyone needs a good mechanic. They're going to beat someone up?"

"Not necessarily. They always try to reason with him. If he's uncooperative then he gets hit. Such is life." Xan took her beer as she got up. "I'm gon' lay down before they come back. It might be a long night."

"Good night." Zoe finished her books and ordered her and Ben's tickets for St. Thomas. They'd be leaving in two days and would be back in four. And in five she'd have the signed contracts in her hands for her stores and all her dreams would be realized.

She wondered if he'd still want to travel with her after she'd told him she couldn't be with him, but instinctively she knew he would. Ben wasn't unprofessional. It was she who'd enticed him. Forcing him to lie with her at her house, then here at his house. And then having a meltdown today. No, she was an emotional basket case.

He never stopped doing his job, including now. Ben was a hired gun. *Her* hired gun and on her command, he beat men up. Men who beat *her* up, her conscience argued. Men who deserved it, and men who worked for Mitchell Turner.

She'd told Ben to kill her attacker, but she hadn't meant it. Hopefully, he wouldn't do anything that drastic. She couldn't imagine being in jail for the rest of her life. Never being able to experience success and joy. Never being able to know the depth of passion, and the way Ben cared for her making her feel special.

Being without Ben for a day had hurt, but made things clearer. It was late and he wasn't home from freeing the world of bad guys. One day the bad guys might get the best of him. Did she really want to spend the rest of her life waiting up for a man who might not come home because he was beating up someone?

Zoe whimpered and opened her eyes. She was still in the kitchen at the table, asleep. It was two in the morning and she was waiting for Ben.

The house had fallen into silence with only house sounds to keep her company. The tick of the clock, the faint hum of her computer fan and the occasional hiss from the air conditioner when it clicked on, reminded her that she wasn't home.

Zoe sighed as she packed her computer bag, headed down the hall to the white eyelet room. She opened the door and Ben's sister Mel was already asleep.

She softly closed the door and headed to the living room where she saw Xan stretched out asleep, her arm over her eyes.

Ben's leather recliner didn't look inviting at all.

Zoe took the stairs slowly, knowing that she was heading to his bedroom, hearing her words to him and Rob. She remembered the pain that had seared her chest and her hands as Ben had squeezed, and the tenderness in his lips when she'd kissed him.

She knew why she'd said she couldn't be with him. They were getting sloppy and she didn't want him or her to die for love.

Zoe squeezed her eyes shut as she pulled the comforter off the bed and threw it and a pillow on the thickly carpeted floor.

She was in love with the man helping her, but she could never, ever tell him. She'd been married before, and she knew the end result of marriage was a terrible divorce so why would she fall in love again?

She was smart in business, but in affairs of the heart, not. She wrapped herself in the blanket and let her body download. She conjured up Charles' words and the pain she'd been in. Once she found it, she imagined sticking her toe in and feeling the burn before immersing her foot all the way to her calf….

Love was like cancer. She vowed to remember that as she went to sleep.

Chapter 21

"Tell me why you have to go with Zoe to St. Thomas when we know Turner is our guy? Cooke confirmed it."

"Because the case isn't solved."

Ben sat in the backseat, hating that Cooke had gotten the jump on him with that beer bottle. He could feel blood oozing out. He might need a few stitches. Nothing Xan couldn't handle.

"We don't know why he's after Zoe, Rob. That missing link is somewhere in St. Thomas. You said yourself, you've been over her books, in her stores and there's nothing extraordinary going on. There's no reason for him to want what she's got, so maybe she hasn't gotten it yet."

Zach came to a complete stop at a stop sign, waited two seconds and then took off. The time reflected three in the morning, and they were three black men driving through

Atlanta. That was enough to get them stopped and questioned by the police.

"I know I said that, but Turner keeps coming back for more. My concern is for you. How long will you be gone?" Rob still didn't sound convinced.

"Three, four days max. She signs the contract on Monday and we confront Turner Monday night. Job over."

"Hugh had some updates," Rob continued. "Gordo couldn't really give a good description of the woman that impersonated Zoe except to say she was tall and not the Zoe he saw at the carnival."

Ben nodded. "What else?"

Zach slowed when he saw the hot sign at the Krispy Kreme donut shop.

"Don't even think about it," Rob told him.

"What we gon' do to Turner?" Zach wondered, his eyes bright, as he passed the shop. "I love those rich types. They start begging and making deals. 'I can make this work for the both of us,'" he imitated. "You know they'd stab you in the heart if you didn't have their balls in a nut cracker. God, that's so much fun."

Ben and Rob chuckled at their brother. "You need a girlfriend," Ben told him.

"I keep getting turned down."

"Tell me about it," Ben said.

"You're lucky. Zoe's into you."

"She's scared of me. She had a crazy ex-husband who took her money. I'd keep her in a heartbeat."

Rob turned around to look at him. "You're lying."

"Nope."

"You've known her two months," Rob informed him.

"And she's never complained about me not practicing law even though I have a law degree. She doesn't complain that my feet stink, or that you guys are always in my house. She doesn't want a dog, and she's not trying to get married tomorrow. Neither am I."

"That's all it takes?" Rob asked him.

"Hell, I'd date you," Zach said, looking over his shoulder.

"Watch the road," Ben and Rob said at the same time.

"That's not all it'd take, but it's a good beginning. I want her, Rob. I'm falling in love with her and I like that. But she doesn't know and I'm going to keep it that way. She has to love me on her own accord or else it won't work."

"You'd better know what you're getting into before you commit to her. You still might fall short in her eyes and you'll get hurt."

"And I can get hurt trying to live a safe life, too, Rob."

Zach turned onto Ben's driveway and drove one-tenth of a mile around the curve to the side of the house and got out of the car. Zoe's car hadn't been moved in days and it looked lonely in the dark corner, lit by moonlight. They started toward the door when Rob pulled his gun.

Zach and Ben followed suit. "What?"

"No lights."

Ben realized what his brother was talking about. The driveway lights hadn't come on, nor had the side porch lights. They'd been installed for security purposes.

"Would somebody be stupid enough to come here and try something?"

Zach had voiced Ben's exact thoughts.

Ben's heart hammered against his ribs, and he couldn't think straight. Zoe was inside somewhere and so were his sisters. Xan and Mel were more able to take care of themselves, but Zoe—she was another story.

"I'm going around back," Zachary signed.

For his size, six-four two hundred forty pounds, Zach

was as agile as a cat. He scaled the porch and deck, which didn't please Ben until Zach got to the balcony and let himself in.

Seconds later he backed out, Zoe's gun inches from his face.

"Ben, she might be sleepwalking. I don't think she knows it's me."

Twenty feet below he could see Zach's hands up and Zoe's arm extended, the gun aimed to kill.

"Zoe, baby. It's my brother Zachary. Stand down, sweetheart."

"He doesn't know how to use the stairs?"

"Yes, he does, but the lights didn't come on outside. We thought there might be a problem."

"Zachary, you scared me. I don't like surprises," she told him, and pulled the gun down.

Zach coughed in relief. "I swear to God, I'll never, ever surprise you again." He looked over the deck at Ben. "Bruh, she's one firecracker. I'm coming down."

"Take the stairs."

"Hell no! If I go back in there, she might really shoot me."

Ben sat on a bar stool in the kitchen and got stitched up while Zoe stood in the doorway, ten feet away, watching. "Is that sanitary?" she asked.

"I've done this in tents from Mozambique to Kenya, to the Super Dome in New Orleans. This kitchen is probably the cleanest."

"You can come in," Ben said softly.

"No, thank you."

Mel looked at her and grunted. "You're such a girl."

"I won't deny that." Zoe looked defensive and Ben gave Mel the eye to shut up.

"Why are the outside lights off?" Ben asked his sisters.

"I didn't notice," Mel said.

"Nobody was here but us. Nothing unusual happened either." Xan pulled the thread through, tied and cut it before taping him. "Check the lights tomorrow and see if anything weird happened."

"I'll do that first thing." Rob looked as if he were going to pass out from exhaustion.

Zoe loved the Hoods, she realized, so different than how she'd felt earlier that day, even though she didn't like their occupations. Right now she was scared out of her mind and if she went all the way into the kitchen, she might burst into tears, and they'd all start laughing.

Rob, Zach and Ben looked like they'd been in a bar fight. They were disheveled and a little bloody. Ben's hands seemed to have taken the most abuse, or given it, she realized, and were swollen. His shoulder was gashed, and the chest that she'd always found so sexy, looked unappealing in front of his family.

Zach sat at the table with pillows under his head, asleep, his hand in a bowl of ice. He started snoring and Mel rubbed his back. They all understood each other so well, and they weren't afraid. Mel gently squeezed Zach's shoulder and he quieted.

"I'm going back to bed. Y'all did good tonight. Three stitches? You ought to be ashamed of yourself," Mel said to Ben, and kissed his forehead. "How'd he get the jump on you?"

Ben shrugged. "I don't know."

Everyone froze as if that was a foreign answer, when before he'd said it was okay not to know something. Mel looked sheepishly at Zoe and quickly looked away. "Okay. I'm turning in. Night."

Rob shook Zach, who mumbled himself awake. "What?"

"Come on. Time to go."

They filed past Zoe, saying nothing. Xan put a small bandage on Ben's shoulder and waved them away. "I'm going to be down here for a while cleaning up, so you two go ahead and turn in."

"Good night." Zoe had no choice but to go upstairs with Ben. He'd see that she'd been sleeping on the floor, and he'd have something to say, but her mind was made up. Continuing to be with him was a bad idea. She just didn't fit in because she was afraid.

Zoe held open and then closed the bedroom door behind Ben, knowing he took in the condition of his bed in a glance. The light was on in the bathroom and Ben kicked off his shoes, then walked over to the sitting room and dropped into the chair.

"It's Mitchell Turner. He's after you. Wants to take over your stores and your designs."

"What? Why?" Shocked, Zoe stood in place wanting to go to him, wanting to go to Turner and strangle him for what he'd put her through. "He can hire the best designers in the world. I'm small potatoes in Atlanta."

"Maybe not to him. Where do you get your designs?"

"I design them with friends in the Caribbean."

"You told me and Rob at our initial meeting your business has tripled. I'm sure he knows this. If this continues, he likely sees a cash cow. Every business is looking for the next great thing. You might just be it."

The thought had never occurred to her. She'd worked hard to be different and had seen overnight successes, so to speak, in the clothing business, but never in jewelry. But all it took was the right attention on a piece and the business could change with the blink of an eye. The thought had always been a dream of hers, had been what she'd worked so hard for. To have someone steal that away was unbelievable.

"I'm scared now more than ever, Ben. If he takes my stores and my designers, I'll have nothing."

"That's probably what he wants. Everything for himself. But we don't know everything for sure. That's just what Cooke says. We'll know more after we thoroughly investigate. Get some sleep. The team will work on this tomorrow."

"Do you need help with your pants?" she asked him.

Zoe wanted to put her arms around him and thank God he was all right, and then hit him for getting hurt. Her hands ached to touch him all over and search him for other wounds, because he'd done all of this for her. He was so brave and heroic, and yet she felt an anger so deep she wanted to scream.

"I can help you," she said, and started toward him.

"No, I can do it. This is nothing."

The wall of her emotions cracked. "It might be nothing for you, but I don't get stitched up every day. I don't know people that beat up other people and have to get stitches in the kitchen. I don't know what I'm supposed to say right now or what I'm supposed to do."

"What's wrong with you?"

"You're a thug."

Ben patted her chest, and she felt it roll through her body. "Go to bed, Zoe."

"I'm sorry. I don't mean it that way." Zoe felt the tears come and couldn't stop them. "I'm sorry. I know you did this for me and that I sound ungrateful. You've been so good to me—so please accept my apology. Say you forgive me."

"I forgive you. Now go to bed."

"Please come lie down."

"No. I'm going to sit here for a while."

"Ben, I want you to be comfortable." She tugged him by the hand. "Please. I won't believe you've forgiven me for the awful thing I said. Please?"

"Okay," he took slow steps past the bed and lay down on the floor.

"Won't you be more comfortable on the bed?"

"No."

Zoe pushed her hair behind her ear and wiped her eyes. She knelt and pulled off Ben's socks, took off his belt and he slid off his jeans. She got close to him, pulled up the blanket and fell into a dark dreamless sleep.

Morning shone brightly through the balcony doors and Zoe slept on her back, dreams and reality keeping her between two worlds. In her dream she was aware of the morning sun, but also that she was in her store with Mitchell Turner.

The new emblem, the gold Z, had been hung, the counters and carpeting installed, yet he wasn't happy and kept taking jewelry out of the case and hiding it behind his back. Every time she'd ask him for it, he'd show her his empty hands.

She'd turn around to complete the tour and just when he thought she wasn't looking, he'd steal more jewelry.

Frustrated, she pushed him.

"Hey, what are you dreaming about?"

Zoe awoke sitting up, her hands on her face. She looked at both sides of her hands, then wondered why she and Ben were on the floor. Their night came flooding back. "Oh, goodness. Last night—"

"You tripped out on me."

She remembered crying and begging him to forgive her. Oh, goodness. Holding a gun on Zachary. She covered her face and wanted to lie back down and sleep the memories away, but she had to face reality.

Being in love didn't have to hurt so badly or come at such a high price. It was the pretending she wasn't in love that was so hurtful. "I owe you an explanation, Ben. I was worried about you a little too much."

"There's never too much worrying about me. I appreciate that you care."

Zoe was glad that her hair disguised her face. Caring was an understatement. If only he knew. Ben tugged on her collar.

"I thought we had to get going?" she said to him.

"It's not even seven yet. We've got a few minutes. Wait, I'll be back."

Ben got up and used the bathroom, and Zoe used the hallway bathroom, beating him back by a minute. He got back down on the floor with her and tucked her in.

"What are you doing?" Zoe asked when he started playing with her hair with one hand, and rubbing the palm of his other hand over her nipple. Through the thin material of her shirt, her nipple bloomed. Her body wasn't a liar. There was no denying the pleasure Ben gave her.

"I'm prolonging the night," he finally told her.

"It's morning."

His face was in her neck, his five-o'clock shadow causing her to grow wetter as he caressed her shoulder. Zoe hadn't known this was an erogenous zone before him.

"I don't believe it's morning," he whispered as he moved to her other breast. "You're not wearing your pajamas."

"You had this on the other day and it—never mind." Zoe pulled her feet up.

"Tell me." Ben curled his legs under her butt and pulled her legs over his thighs. He was creating a sensual mood she almost couldn't resist.

"I put it on because it smelled like you. I was worried you wouldn't come back."

"Baby, I always come back. Didn't my sisters tell you that?"

"I didn't say anything to them."

"What did you do all night?"

"Balanced the books from both stores. I had a record-setting day with the help of your sisters."

"So you worried all night long?" He knew her better than ever. His palm skimmed her nipple again causing shivers to race through her torso. Zoe gripped him with her thighs, but couldn't meet his gaze. "That feels good," he said. "I like that you care about me." He stroked her side, bringing her so close to him she could feel his heart beat.

"I was a basket case. I hate that feeling." She'd asked for forgiveness and loved being in his arms now. Making up was so much better, but she was trying to stay focused and save her business. Her meltdown yesterday meant something. She couldn't go backward. "We need to get up."

"Wait a second. Lie back," he said against her back.

Halfway up, Zoe could feel Ben looking at her and she wanted to stay with him. All night she'd slept comfortably beside him, her bottom tucked into his pelvis, and she'd wanted to be with him and nowhere else. In the night, when he'd moved she had, too, loving the way the hairs on his legs felt against her legs.

He ran his fingers through her hair. "Baby, stay with me."

Zoe lay down and Ben ripped the shirt, causing the buttons to scatter. He devoured her breasts, making her nether region throb when he pressed himself against her. All the love she had in her heart surfaced.

"Ben, this is so bad," she said, breathless. "What will happen to me if something happens to you?"

"Stop, baby," he murmured.

She kissed him, loving the fullness of his mouth and

how it felt now, first thing in the morning. Truthfully, it could have been lunch time or midnight and Ben could make her feel good just by kissing her. He was right, nothing about him was bad, and if she didn't put an end to what was happening now, they wouldn't stop because she had no resistance to him. She turned away, so she could get up. "Now, Ben—"

He ran his hand over her pantiless bottom and worked it between her legs. Speechless, she opened wider, letting pleasure take her higher.

"Don't say no," he said against her back. "Don't fight it." He sucked on her shoulder where the shirt had fallen away and she leaned back, her legs trembling.

With his fingers inside her and his thumb on her clit working in tandem, she went off like New Year's Eve fireworks.

Pulling her on top of him, Zoe sat on his lap, her arms around his neck. She wanted him to feel like she did, close and loved and wanted. Holding him, she submitted to his strokes, her body rocking from the pleasure. "Ben," she gasped. He was trying to send her there again.

Zoe couldn't stop kissing him, her feelings tumbling out. Each time her hand passed over the bandage on his shoulder, she kissed him more deeply, wanting him to know how much she loved him.

She pushed him against the bed letting her hands say what words couldn't.

When he turned the tables and put her half on the bed, her body began to tremble. Ben plunged into her and she cried out, clawing at the sheets, contractions hitting her body in waves. Ben turned her over, his strength amazing, his hand holding her at her shoulder and neck, moving down to her breasts as he pushed her further onto the bed.

"Tell me," he said.

"What?"

"What's in your eyes."

Zoe wished she was on her stomach again so her feelings weren't so well known. She reached for him. Ben didn't usually let her bring him close. This time he did. He stayed inside her and she gazed at him. "I'm in love with you and it scares me."

"Don't be scared to love me, Zoe."

He moved in her. "I really do, Ben." She lifted her hips, seeking him at a greater depth. Saying it aloud pushed her closer.

Zoe hadn't had to speak aloud. Her body had said everything for her.

But her dark clouds still loomed.

Chapter 22

The flight to St. Thomas was filled with honeymooners and vacationers. Ben sat in the aisle seat, while Zoe hugged the window, her chin braced on her hand, staring out. She'd been lost in her own world since they'd boarded nearly an hour and a half ago, and he wondered when she'd give up on the silent treatment. They'd made love hours ago and now this?

"We have to talk sometime, Zoe."

She shook her head and crossed her legs, sticking her hand between her knees. She wanted to put as much distance between them as possible it seemed.

"Is this how you resolve all your problems, because I'm starting to see a pattern. You never want to talk about anything that might get into your heart."

"Ben, please let me work this out."

"Work what out, Zoe? Be honest and tell me that much."

Zoe looked up at the movie playing on the screen.

When she did look at him there was a storm brewing. "You worked for me, and I made your job difficult by becoming sexually involved with you. I compromised our safety by letting my heart rule my head. I blamed you for not stopping danger that was being directed toward me, when you've only tried to protect me, and I threatened your brother with a gun. Moreover, I'm afraid for your safety all the time, and I wonder if I can ever have a relationship with a man who does what you do, and I can't find an answer to that question.

"I never thought I'd find the perfect man for me. In my business, I call it the perfect solitaire. We're always looking for the perfect diamond. I've never found or seen one. You're the perfect diamond in the rough, you're right here, and I realized that I can't have you because you're everything that scares me. I'm not angry, I'm sad."

"The captain has turned on the Fasten Seatbelt sign as we prepare for landing. Please turn off your electrical devices and stow your carry-ons. We should be on the ground in five minutes," the flight attendant said.

Her gaze never wavered the entire time the announcement was made.

"You can't live your life afraid, Zoe. Me loving you doesn't require you to do anything drastic. It's not an action item on a to-do list."

She rejected his words with a violent shake of her head. "Love doesn't work." Her eyes were misty as she turned away and looked out the window.

"So you love me, too? Zoe, that isn't a bad thing."

Zoe nodded her head and crossed her arms. "I'm not going to do anything about it, Ben. The subject is closed."

Couples around them nuzzled one another, happy to be in love.

Ben couldn't understand why he and Zoe were the only miserable couple in love on the plane.

Holly and William greeted Zoe with a warmth and affection that Zoe responded to without hesitation. This was the family she was missing, the family she deserved. Not the absent mother who never called to check on her, or the cold mean sister who was so jealous she'd steal from her sister for her own selfish gain.

William and Holly doted on Zoe, commenting on her weight loss and how much her hair had grown. They talked about her pretty skin and Holly wondered why her eyes looked sad, and then she looked over Zoe's shoulder.

Ben smiled and extended his hand. William shook Ben's hand first. "I'm William, Brudah. You look like jus de man for Zoe."

Ben wanted to agree. "She has a lot to say about that. It's nice to meet you. I love St. Thomas."

William turned a bright smile to Zoe. "Yes! Yeees! Zoe, he loves my native land and you do, too? My gurl, dis is da man. Come. We got a lot ta do."

Holly was young and beautiful like Zoe, dark and thin, with a wide smile and easy manner Ben could tell was genuine. She strolled alongside Zoe, completely relaxed in her white tank top and long blue skirt, in complete contrast to her taller friend who looked sexy but serious in a red two-piece pant suit.

Zoe had straightened all the curls out of her hair and put it in a bun, the worst hairstyle Ben had ever seen on a woman, and wore straight earrings, not the hoops that he liked that she'd been wearing.

Holly sized up Ben as he and William stowed the

luggage in the trunk outside baggage claim. "Gurl, you know how ta pick 'em. I'm Holly."

Zoe looked uncomfortable.

Ben shook Holly's hand. "Nice to meet you. How far do you live from here?"

"You're just like Zoe when she first came from the States. Always in a rush to get everywhere. Don't worry about how far I live," she teased. "Enjoy yourself. You'll get where you got ta go when you get der."

Zoe looked at Ben's shirt. "She's giving you a hard time because she likes you. They live twenty minutes from here."

"I see we're going to be best friends, Holly," Ben told her. "I have two sisters who love to give me a hard time."

"Welcome to de family," William told him as he shoved the last bag into the jeep and eyed Ben who was taller than his lean five-foot-seven frame. "If you jus friends with dat woman, den you might as well be dead. She too fine to jus be shaking hands wit."

Ben laughed and pounded fists with William. "You're right about that."

Holly and Zoe got in the back, talking, and the men got in front.

"We goin' straight to the shop, Zoe. I got a lot for you to see. Did you bring the stones?"

"Yes, my dear. I got everything you need."

William navigated the clogged streets with ease, cutting corners and traveling side roads.

He was a wealth of information about the island and the jewelry business, offering his knowledge without hesitation. He explained that there was only one black jeweler in St. Thomas now among all the jewelers. Most were from India, China or the States. William used to design for them, but he didn't anymore because his designs had been copied and his prices undercut, so he'd gone out on his own and had linked up with Zoe three years ago. They'd been doing well so far, but he was confident the new designs would change their worlds.

Ben asked William to show him the business who'd done this to him. They drove by Tyrique Designs and Ben asked William to stop. The building was beige with columns in the front. Tall guards stood outside and opened the doors for customers. They didn't smile or greet people. They simply opened and closed the doors.

"I wouldn't advise you goin' inside without buying nothing," William told him, letting him out down the street.

"You can't force a person to buy. I'm a tourist and I'll buy if I want to. I'll be back."

"Ben, don't take any unnecessary chances," Zoe told him, her hand on his shoulder.

"Baby, that's what I do."

Ben went inside and knew it was a Mitchell Turner operation. At the desk near the back of the boutique, he spotted the same chair he'd had in his office in Duluth, Georgia in the back office. Ben strolled through the store, noting the design and set up. What did Turner want from Zoe? Ben knew if he had the answer to that question, he could nail Turner to the wall.

Ben finally exited, a small bag in hand and gave it to Zoe.

"What's this?" she asked, opening the bag.

"Did you know that perfume can damage jewelry if you spray it directly on a piece repeatedly?"

"Yes, I know."

"I bought it just to see the sales team at work," he said.

"Brudah, don't mess with dem. They want to bury us."

"Bad blood?"

"No blood," William said with a frown. "He don't even

come over here no more. It's owned by some big corporation and nobody can get to the bottom of who it is no more. It sickens me that he comes in and undercuts our prices and steals our designs and sells them for pennies on the dollar."

"You should sue," Ben told him.

"We do, but they tie you up in legal fees for so long, you be dead and broke before they call your case."

"No worries," Holly said from the backseat, her hand on William's shoulder.

He took her hand and kissed it. "You right, Holly Sheba."

"Holly Sheba?" Ben repeated, trying to catch the meaning.

"Holly Queen," William translated for him. "When the queen speaks, the king listens or the king won't survive because he cannot live alone, right, Zoe Sheba?"

She was quiet a few seconds. "Right, William."

They continued through the streets and Ben people watched, enjoying the ride.

Soon the roads thickened with weeds, and patches of land were broken by rows for farmed land. Men and women walked along the roadside, some with staffs in their hands, Ben guessed to ward off animals or snakes.

They wound through the hills until they came to a gated house. William pressed the button and the gate opened, allowing them entry.

The house was gorgeous, but it was the workshop that Ben was most impressed with. He'd been to the garment district in Atlanta and New York. He'd been to studios in California where movies were shot, but he'd never been in a real jewelry workshop where stones were cut into one-of-a-kind pieces.

William and Holly worked well together, talking in a dialect he couldn't fully comprehend, yet he was able to pick up enough to understand that all of their talk wasn't about jewelry, but about him and Zoe.

Zoe waited on the side, away from him, and Ben couldn't stand it any longer. He started toward her and she got this look in her eyes that warned him away. "I'm going back into town to rent a car," he said.

"You're leaving?" She seemed surprised, and Ben was suddenly glad he decided to leave.

"No, he not goin' nowhere. Now that Zoe's here, I don't need my car. Problem solved," William said.

"I need to check on a few things. I'll get our bags and give you some time to get business taken care of." He walked over to her.

"Is everything safe?" she asked, her eyes imploring. Suddenly, she held out her hands and he took them in his.

"I'm going to check it out now. Don't worry. I'm going to do my job."

A tender smile passed across her face, followed closely by regret. "There's never been a doubt in my mind that you were."

"You're safe, Zoe."

"I'll see you later."

He headed toward the door, Zoe behind him, her hand inches from his. Ben slowed when he saw the perfect black stone lying next to a silver chain in a display case. "What is this?"

"A black diamond. A three-carat stone with a white gold necklace. I've got to find the perfect setting so it doesn't fall out. I need something that sets the stone off right. Or I may have to do something else besides a necklace. There's a detectable flaw on the side of the stone. I've got to think about what to do with it."

Ben held it up. "It's the perfect solitaire. A ring is perfect." Ben handed it to her. "It might have a flaw, but that's what makes it unique. It's perfect. Just like you. I'll be back."

196 The Perfect Solitaire

He wanted to kiss her, but he walked away.

Back in the city, Ben went to a couple jewelry stores and talked to store owners who tried everything to entice him to part with his money. When he mentioned shopping at Tyrique's, they worked harder to get his business, but none could match Tyrique's bargain-basement prices. Ben found one black-owned jewelry store where the owner gave him a great price on a pearl and diamond necklace and he bought if for Zoe. He figured he might get in trouble later, but it was beautiful and he wanted to show her he had good taste. He waited for the strand of pearls to be wrapped and watched the sea of tourists stream by and saw a face he recognized.

Debrena had walked off the job a couple weeks ago abandoning Ireland in the Peachtree store. She'd been present the day of Faye's robbery, and she'd been on staff when several other robberies had taken place.

Her hair was styled differently but there was no mistaking it was the same person.

Ben dialed Rob and Zach as he followed her and got a chill at her final destination.

"How's it going down there?" Rob asked.

"We've caught a break. I saw Debrena Cole, one of Zoe's former sales managers. She works for Turner."

"How do you know?" Rob asked.

Ben could hear him typing into his computer.

"She walked into Tyrique's, went behind the counter and then into the back of the store. I'd say that's kind of familiar."

"All right, let's not jump to any conclusions on this one. Zach, are you in?"

"I'm here and just leaving customs. Ben, give me your location."

He gave the street address and a few stores as a reference. You can't miss Turner's store he's got MT under Tyrique Jewelers on the front glass.

"I'm heading back to the house in about an hour. Everything okay back there, Rob?"

"It's good," Rob told him. "That's the first time you've asked about anything else in a while."

"I know. It's been crazy and it's nearly over. Things will return to normal soon."

"What happened between you and Zoe?" Rob asked.

Ben debated how much to tell. "She loves me," he admitted.

"Wow." There was a long pause then Rob said, "Why aren't you the happiest man alive?"

"Because she said she isn't going to do anything about it. I'll call you later."

Ben shadowed Debrena for hours and finally saw Zach across from him and signed that he was dropping his surveillance. Debrena had never met Zach before so Ben hoped she didn't see him and notice the similarities, or they'd be in trouble.

Ben retrieved the car and drove back to the house to find Holly, Zoe and William immersed in talks about the upcoming line. He sat back and watched Zoe, who'd abandoned the red pants and jacket for shorts and a camisole. This was one of the rare times he'd seen her in her element. They were close to ending this whole matter and she'd be able to decide if her life of solitude was what she wanted for her future.

Zoe walked around the tables and showed William how she wanted the new diamond bracelets to look. She'd unwound her hair from that uptight bun to a loose ponytail that hung straight down her back and hugged the maid who served dinner while they continued to meet.

They went from the computer to the tables a hundred times. "We need a moderate price point that lures the working woman who earns under fifty thousand dollars."

"No, Zoe," William said. "You should be known for the black diamonds and chocolate diamonds. Holly brought me some ideas of what's sellin' in the States, and we can beat all the designers if we do something with copper and black diamonds."

"William, that's hot. Holly, I must have missed you when you were in the States."

William walked through his large expanse of tables, the diamond in his hand. "What you talking 'bout, gurl? She stay wit you."

Zoe immediately banged herself in the forehead. "William, forgive me. I'm going crazy. The attack made me forget things."

Holly and Ben were opposite one another and she looked terrified as she stood rooted in place.

"When were you attacked?" William asked, coming toward Zoe.

"Several weeks ago. Ben's been taking care of me since."

"I'm so sorry to hear that, Zoe Sheba. Have you fully recovered?"

"I'm nearly there. Please don't worry."

"No," he said, his hands to his mouth. "We must stop for the evening. I heard nothing about this. Ben is tired. I am truly sorry, Zoe Sheba. We will get a late start tomorrow to give us a long night of rest. We've much to accomplish this week. Go, Zoe Sheba. The night is over."

Zoe protested. "William, please. I'm fine. Ben, tell him. We're not tired, are we?"

Ben walked over, took Zoe's hand and squeezed. "Yes, we're tired, darling."

Zoe met his gaze for the first time that day and so many emotions played out in his eyes. She knew it was time to wrap things up. "Okay. Enough for tonight."

"Zoe, we put you in the bungalow because of flooding in the room from last week's storm. Come, your bags are already der."

Holly led the way with William following closely. The women turned around.

"William, what are you doing?" Zoe asked him. "You don't have to come down with us."

"No problem, Zoe Sheba." His gaze was fixed on Holly. "I'm jus making sure my guests are comfortable."

They entered the bungalow that was built like a comfortable guest beach house with a small living room, a kitchenette, a bathroom and two small bedrooms. Ben was glad there were two bedrooms. He didn't want Zoe to think he was going to pressure her to do anything she didn't want to.

"We'll be just fine," Zoe told William. "Holly, are there any women's products in the bathroom?"

"I think so. Let me check."

The two strolled off and Ben and William waited in the living room.

"I can't lose her," William said to Ben.

"Then don't act like you have."

It was dark out and the mosquito netting had already been pulled down. The air conditioner hummed cooling the bungalow so that they'd be comfortable for the evening. Ben was tired, having slept little and on the floor, but he hoped to rest that night.

William looked frustrated and angry, but Ben was more curious as to why she'd lie.

Zoe walked back into the room first followed by Holly. "Good night, William. Night, Holly."

Holly took William's hand and kissed him. His posture softened. He would forgive her. "Night, love," Holly said, and they left.

Chapter 23

Zoe prepared for bed wondering why she hadn't chosen different pajamas when she'd packed. She looked at the sheer white and pink teddies in her hands and realized that they were two of the ones Ben had selected from her house. They left little to the imagination.

But she didn't have anything else, and she couldn't go into his room and take one of his shirts. She sat on the end of the bed, staring into her suitcase. How had she gotten herself into this? Everything in her wanted to be with him. She rubbed the back of her neck and could feel his hand replacing hers, easing away the tension. She even imagined herself falling asleep in the comfort of his arms. But she wasn't a baby, she was an adult and she couldn't go back on her word.

She stood and tightened her shoulders then relaxed them, and abandoned the idea of pajamas, keeping her clothes on. Ben was in the other room waiting to talk to her.

She walked into the kitchenette for a bottle of water, found wine and poured a glass for herself. "Wine?" she offered.

"No. Why was Holly in Atlanta and didn't call you?" he asked, all business. This was what she'd asked for, but certainly not what her disappointed heart expected.

"She told me she was thinking about moving and didn't want to put me in the middle of their personal crisis."

"Do you believe her?"

"I have no reason not to." Zoe drank her wine wishing it was something stronger.

"You don't think this has anything to do with the attacks on you and the fact that they're your top jewelry designers?"

"No. She said she found a place, but she and William are working on things, so I don't think they're breaking up. They seem content."

"Where's the place she was looking at? Did she say?"

"In Smyrna."

"And you believe her?"

"Yes, Ben, I do." Zoe sipped the wine, growing more uncomfortable with his flat affect and the coolness of his manner.

"This is what I hear. Holly came all the way to the States and found an apartment in Smyrna, Georgia, twenty-five minutes from you. She didn't call you, but used you as an alibi to her husband, who you're friends with. She lied and said she stayed with you, and put you in a position where you had to either lie for her or cause an uncomfortable scene between a husband and wife. Holly resembles you, and the mystery of the imposter Zoe McKnight is still unsolved. Holly was in town about that time, so, is she the mysterious Zoe McKnight? Finally, why does Mitchell Turner seem to know your every move?"

The chardonnay soured on her tongue, and she set the glass on the counter. His words hit her hard, pounding her point of judgment, causing her to doubt her decisions. This felt like a personal failure. Holly was her betrayer? Was it possible the person she'd kept the closest was the one who'd hurt her the most? Zoe couldn't and wouldn't believe that of Holly. She had to find a way to help Ben and to help herself.

"Ben, I just don't know. I wouldn't think it of her. Did you find out anything else?"

"I spotted Debrena in town and we're following that angle, as well."

"So she could be the link. I won't believe Holly had anything to do with hurting me."

Ben nodded and came toward her.

Zoe could feel her body preparing to be taken by him although her mind said no. He had changed into shorts and a tank top, his muscles bulging from beneath the cool-gray T-shirt. "I'm turning in. The place is all locked up. Good night." He walked around her into his dark room, got on top of the bed and lay down.

Zoe stood alone in the center of the living room feeling like a fool. "Good night."

Zoe awoke with a headache and a bad attitude. She drank coffee and wished the heat would give way to a breeze. Ben was gone by the time she got up and dressed and she headed up to the house alone. "Have you seen Ben?"

"He left early," Holly told her, looking exhausted. "All is fine with me and William. We made up all night long. You should make up with Ben."

"What makes you think we're broken up?"

"He went jogging at six in the morning," Holly said,

laughing. "Any satisfied man would be asleep with his mouth open, snoring. That tells me you didn't do a good job."

Zoe chuckled, watching her friend closely. "It's complicated."

"Der's no expiration on happiness. It comes when we need it. You lucky. Don't waste your chance, gurl."

"I need something for this headache," Zoe said, the hot drink and caffeine not helping.

Holly gave her a rueful gaze. "I can't give you dat. You'd better call ya man."

They both fell out laughing.

"Holly, walk with me."

They stepped outside and followed the path down to the water. "What were you doing in Atlanta?"

"I knew dis was going to come up. I was der seeing a breast specialist. I did a breast exam and found a lump and needed to see a specialist. Miami is a great place, but I love Atlanta. They have great doctors, too, so I went der."

Zoe was surprised and stopped short.

Holly pulled a paper from her skirt pocket and gave it to Zoe. "All is well. I wanted ta show it ta you after yesterday. But you see, no cancer."

Relief and happiness swept her. "Why didn't you tell me?"

"Because you have your own life and problems, Zoe Sheba, and William and I were having our own life and problems. Sometimes a man needs ta wonder what his woman is doing to bring him back ta himself and ta der relationship. All is well, as I said. We are fine."

"Does William know about the lump?"

"No, but I believe I proved my love ta him many times last night." They laughed and held hands all the way back up to the house.

William came in looking happy and content and kissed his wife.

"Zoe, you ready to work?"

"Yes," she said. "Let's get to it."

Debrena moved through the streets of St. Thomas and ate her lunch at a small Internet café, where she didn't use the computers but picked up papers and studied them before making calls on her cell phone. Ben signed to Zach they needed to pick her up before she got back to work or they'd lose their chance for the day. Just as she entered the alley, the block-long shortcut to her job, they snatched her and pulled her into their car.

After the initial shock, she didn't resist being strapped in.

"You don't look surprised to see us." Zack settled next to her in the paneled van, that Ben drove in circles to make sure they weren't being followed.

"Is anyone ever?"

"You can give us what we want now or your life can become very uncomfortable," he told her.

"You don't kill people," she retorted, "so I'm not scared of you."

Zach held up his phone and snapped her picture. "Do you work for Mitchell Turner?"

She rolled her eyes. "Kiss my behind."

Zach laughed and pressed Send on his phone. "I'll have old Mitch verify your employment himself."

The phone vibrated and Debrena started to shake. "You're trying to get me killed! Is that him? He's going to kill me!"

Zach shrugged. "Should have answered me." He pressed the button. "He uses flowery language, but confirms that you work for him."

Ben drove into the hills to an abandoned house Zach had found.

"How long have you worked for Turner?"

"Two years," she said, her bravado weakening like Maine tourists in the Caribbean heat. "You've got to help me."

Zach attached cuffs to the woman, who barely reached five foot four. But he was smart. They didn't need any more surprises. "Why would we want to do that? You're a liar and a thief. Zoe was beaten up and her stores robbed. Why would we want to help you?"

"I'm no different from Zoe. I did what I had to do. I'm a woman who is trying to take care of her family. Now that you've busted me, what's going to happen to my children? Turner will kill me."

Zach shrugged and Ben knew it was all part of the act. "Lady," he said, "you give us what we want and we'll consider it."

"I've been his inside person for two years. He not only wanted her stores, but the copyright for the floor safe she'd invented."

Ben knew Debrena was holding back. "There's got to be more to it."

"As the protection on Zoe and her home grew tighter, his frustration heightened. He knew she was coming here, so I was sent to find her designers," she told Ben. "Turner's been obsessed with her ever since you came into the picture. His desire is to dominate the jewelry business in Atlanta. Her designs are becoming so hot, he wanted to control her and have her indebted to him by owning her stores and making her work for him."

"So he wants her?"

"Yes, he wants Zoe, but he wants her business, too. He's greedy."

"Did you get what you came for?"

"Yes." Debrena tried to look tough, but Ben knew she was lying.

"How?" He pushed.

"I followed you home last night."

Zach laughed in Debrena face and dialed. "You're lying. I've been following you, and you were never close. Mitchell Turner, please. Who am I? Tell him the photo I just e-mailed him—well, his friend has been talking."

"No," she whisper-shouted. "Okay, I'm lying. Hang up." She waited, her eyes pleading.

Zachary hung up. "That's your last lie. You understand?"

Debrena nodded. "I haven't found Zoe yet, but I'm getting close. If you caught me, that means she's nearby. She's never far from you, Ben. She's in the hills, I know. I know her friend Holly is a designer, but she's a hermit and hardly ever comes to town."

An uneasy feeling grew inside Ben and he wanted to call Zoe. "You stole her date book? That's how you knew about her meeting here in St. Thomas?"

"Yes, but Zoe wasn't good at updating her calendar, so I had to break in to her house. That was simple. I took the keys from her father while he was in the hospital, and I returned them right before Zoe took them for her meeting with you. Anybody can dress up like a nurse. Accessing her computer wasn't easy. Her password is so complicated we couldn't break it, so I had to go back to the store one night. Zoe came back for her purse, and things got hairy. She almost got killed."

"For jewelry, Debrena?"

"No, Ben," she retorted, cocky. "For the money and the power. Turner wants everyone to corner the market in one industry. He wants to do that here in Atlanta. If there's any unique entity out there, he'll destroy them so he can be number one. As for me, it's insulting to work for ten dollars an hour when food and gas are twice as expensive. I work for Turner because he pays well. Turner likes vintage cars, and I like to eat and feed my kids."

"Who has the jewelry and the money that was stolen from Zoe's stores?" Zach asked.

"Turner, but he sold a necklace online. He tried to get it back, but the guy can't be located. I suspected you Hoods were involved, but I couldn't prove anything, so I kept my mouth shut," she answered, stamping her feet at the crawling things on the floor, though she couldn't move too much with her arms restrained behind her back. "I was given a bonus for the total amount brought in. A nice percentage."

"You impersonated Zoe," Ben said, hoping it wasn't Holly.

"That was simple: I needed the money, and to this day neither Zoe nor Turner knows about that."

"So there's no middleman for Turner," Ben asked, relieved.

"No. Turner's not selling any of her jewelry. He keeps it as trophies. He fell in love with the O'Sullivan collection. I have to check in with him or he'll know something is wrong, and then there'll be hell to pay."

Her eyes shifted and left and Ben knew she was lying. Zach pressed down on her handcuffs and she squealed. "Too bad you're still a liar, Debrena," Zach told her. "You're cute. You'd better start writing your check. You're not calling anybody."

Ben called Rob and replayed the entire incident as he drove back to William and Holly's. "Rob, I don't like this. This feels bigger. I think Turner is here. Rob, he's got a thing for Zoe and he's not going to leave it up to a store clerk to close the deal. Can you call there? No one is answering the phones."

Ben recited the number and waited. Rob came back quickly.

"Ben, Zoe's in trouble. She used the code you told her. She asked for her test results from Dr. Howard. Zach, are you on?"

Zach didn't come back immediately.

Ben pulled off the road and into the brush to conceal the jeep. He removed two firearms he'd concealed in the vehicle and started hiking, affixing the phone to his ear so he could hear Rob give instructions.

"Ben, I've dispatched Hugh to Turner's home here in Atlanta, and I'm going to call Stony over at the junkyard and see if I can borrow the rig. If Turner wants to play with diamonds, we're going to play with his cars, and then we're going to take his money."

"Excellent. Was Zoe able to say how many people were in the house?"

"She said she's elated to be having triplets. And she'll keep her regular appointment in three weeks."

"Three in the house and three out."

"That's good, Ben," Rob said. "She asked about prenatal vitamins and then a male voice told her the news was disappointing, and it was time to get off the phone. She said her friends were going to be sorry they missed hearing about the babies and the phone went dead."

"He separated William and Holly from Zoe. It sounds as if Turner is up there himself. Debrena said he was obsessed with Zoe and he wants money and power. I thought Holly was involved, but she isn't. Zach, get up here. I'm a tenth of a mile on foot. Rob, did Stony get the rig?"

"Stand by," Rob told him.

Ben climbed through the brush and got a call from Zach. "What?"

"I'm at the bottom of the road."

"I drove my car into the brush twenty yards northeast. I'm on foot and can see the house above me. She's right, there are three in the house, three out, they're armed. If I shoot them, it'll be a mess getting off this island."

Rob came back. "Ben, Zach, can you hear me?"

"I copy," Ben said.

"I copy," Zach added.

"We got the rig and will be at Turner's mansion in twenty minutes," Rob informed them.

"Make it ten and take the camera. I want Turner to see what you're doing to his precious cargo. Zach, get up here. I'm going in."

"Ben, you wait for back up," Rob ordered.

"He'd better get here," was all Ben said.

Ben worked his way to the top of the property and didn't see any guards. He knew Zoe wouldn't have been mistaken and wouldn't have given false information. He heard sucking noises as if someone was calling a dog and spotted William beside an abandoned car that had become over-grown with brush.

Ben silently made his way over to him. "Where's Holly?"

"That rat bastard hit her. She's out cold in the bungalow, but she's alright. Turner's got Zoe. I'm worried. He lowered the shades and I can't see inside anymore."

"Where are his guards?"

William gestured over his shoulder. Three big men were unconscious on the ground behind the car, all tied up.

"Those rat bastards," Ben said.

"They're stupid. They couldn't resist the ganja." He shrugged his shoulders. "We got to get into the house and get Zoe."

"My brother is out there. Don't lure him with your crazy weed. I'm going up."

"Go in through my workshop and up the stairs. If they're in the living room, they won't see you coming. Stay in the bush thirty yards and lift the door, go down and up the stairs."

Ben followed instructions and was in the house in minutes that felt like hours. He listened for Zoe's voice, and heard her trying to reason with Turner.

"Ben left me. He's not out there."

"Then you should have no problem signing over your stores and working for me. You'll be happy. I promise."

"My jewelry designs, my safe copyright and me. That's what this has all been about?"

"That's right, Zoe. Total domination. I want to be the kingpin of the Atlanta jewelry business. The entire Southeast, even! I wanted you, but pregnant with triplets?" He frowned and all his capped teeth showed. "That's damned unattractive. Now I want your stores, and I want your designs. They're innovative and fresh. Better than I've seen in years and that says something in a business full of young copycats and fakes."

"No deal, Mr. Turner."

He spread his hands showing her the empty room. "You're hardly in a position to bargain."

"You're right. I'm not trying to strike a deal. I'm giving you a chance to walk out of here."

He walked closer to her, his stomach protruding. "You're cocky. I don't like that in a woman. I'm giving you one last chance to allow me to make you happy."

"I can't think of anything I'd like less."

Ben removed his gun from the holster and suddenly a shot was fired.

* * *

Ben's arm burned and Zoe's face swam into view.

"What the hell happened?" Ben asked, feeling as if a hot poker had been stabbed into his shoulder. The same one that had been cut by Cooke.

"I didn't even know you were in the house, and he shot you. The partition is nothing but translucent paper. He saw you and shot you, so I beat him up."

"Yeah," Zach said. "By the time I got in here, she'd broken his ribs, an arm, and had his head in a vice grip between her thighs."

Ben rubbed the tears from Zoe's eyes. "Thank you, baby."

"You're welcome," she cried. "Can you sit up?" she maintained the pressure on his wound.

"Not yet. Has anyone seen to Holly?" he asked.

"William's at the bungalow now. We had to call the police. It's pretty much a mess up here," Zach told him.

Ben felt strange looking up at the ceiling. "Zach, how long was I out? Is Turner alive?"

"Two minutes, and yes, and he's going to make it. You are, too."

"Good, because I'm going to kill him. Where is he?"

"Watching TV," Zoe told him, rocking him in her arms, tears streaming down her cheeks. "Oh, baby, oh, baby," she repeated again and again.

Ben knew this was stressful for Zoe, but there was no way Zach would allow the bad guy to be watching TV.

"Zach, clarify what she just said, please."

His brother nodded. "Zoe's right."

"Zoe, let me help him up," Zach told her.

She nodded and scooted to the side.

Zach lifted Ben and helped him walk to the living room where Turner was tied to a chair, watching his vintage cars be crushed. His family had been moved from the house to a hotel and all of the money from his safe was taken.

Rob's mask-covered face came into view. "This money will go back to the store owners that you ripped off. Oh, the 1905 Fiat."

"You don't have to do this," Turner wheezed, his ribs broken by Zoe's vicious kicks. "We can make a deal."

"Didn't I tell you they always say that?" Zach laughed.

"You did," Ben agreed. "But I told him, for every finger of hers, ten of his."

"Not the '56 Camaro." Turner began to cry.

"Shut up!" Zoe walked over to him, her hand raised. "Say something else and I'll chop your head off."

The bad and the good guys waited for the police in silence.

Ben sat up in his bed, his arm on the mend two weeks after leaving St. Thomas. Zoe brought the tray of food upstairs and set it on the bed before climbing in beside him.

"Baby, you don't have to wear your pearl earrings every day."

Zoe glanced at them in the mirror. "Yes, I do. I love them."

He eyed the tray of food, her hair that she wore wild and loose and her big smile. All of the love Zoe had for him showed in everything she was doing. He put down the papers he'd been reading and patted his stomach. "I'm going to get fat if you keep feeding me like this."

She eyed the sirloin, potatoes and vegetables. "I won't let you get fat. We can go out to the yard tomorrow if you feel up to it or maybe to the park for a little while. These July days are so hot though, we'd have to go early. I wouldn't want you to be overcome."

Zoe stopped short and her gaze wandered. Ben knew she was still affected by the level of violence she'd witnessed, but he'd worked to allay her fears. He'd held her during the nights of her tears and night terrors and they'd talked about why Turner wanted to dominate her. She'd ended her deals with him, of course, keeping her two stores here in Atlanta, but was being courted by two exclusive New York companies who'd heard her incredible story and had fallen in love with her designs. She'd have her own stores *and* be carried in the nation's longest, most successful department stores.

Turner was being prosecuted in Georgia and St. Thomas and his money had been privately distributed to those he'd stolen from. He was rotting in a St. Thomas jail at that very moment.

"I think we should go back to your house," Ben said.

"You want me to leave?" Zoe pushed up on her knees, her eyes wide and innocent. He wanted to memorize her beauty and keep it locked in his heart forever.

"No," he said, understanding why she looked slightly confused. "I'm not letting you go." Ben put the tray on the floor, took Zoe's hand and brought her to him. "I might have mentioned that you're my woman forever. I just thought you might want a change of scenery."

She molded her body to his. "And you're mine, Ben. I don't mind being here. I like having your brothers surprising me when I come out of the shower, and having them pop over for dinner, and waking up with Rob looking down at you with this very big-brother expression of worry on his face."

Ben laughed. "Yeah, he won't do that again. His wife was killed and he was worried about me. But I told him to call."

Zoe laughed. "I understand. I know. I know." She kissed his nose. "I don't have a family like that. My sister and I will never be close."

"Baby, don't say that."

"Ben, it's the truth. I've come to that awful conclusion and I have to live with it. I called my mother last night and we talked for four whole minutes. She told me she hadn't called because she knew I was going to be okay, but she didn't think my sister could emotionally handle the whole family turning against her."

Ben's brows furrowed. "She should have supported you anyway."

"I know." Zoe's eyes filled with tears, but they didn't spill over. "But you did, Ben. You never wavered."

"You paid me ten grand, baby."

She tickled his chest lightly. "Really. You believed in me before I knew what was happening. I think I fell in love with you then."

Ben gazed into her eyes. Her love was powerful and sure. "Really?"

Zoe nodded.

"What else?" he asked, unbuttoning his shirt that she wore so much better than he did.

"You make me feel special every time I walk through that door with a tray of food or a briefcase full of work. I know it's been hard recovering from surgery, but you've been so good, and I love that about you."

"Thank you, baby. Rob said you wouldn't leave my side at the hospital."

Her eyes filled again as she shook her head. "I had to make sure they weren't cutting the wrong arm."

Ben laughed, kissing the tops of her breasts. "It was the one that was bleeding."

Zoe purred. "I know, but they make mistakes if you don't tell them."

With his good arm he pulled her leg over his. "I'm glad you cared enough to make sure. I like you this way."

"Mmm," she said. "Very sexy." Zoe closed her eyes for a few minutes and let the distant voices of children serenade them. "Ben?"

"Yes, baby?"

"Where do we go from here?"

"I could roll over and you could climb on top of me. That would be nice."

Zoe looked up at him and bit his chin until he laughed, his chest thumping against hers. "Okay, sorry. I suppose you want a serious answer."

"Yes, please."

"We had a very sexy beginning. Hot and heavy and sexy," he said, kissing her nose. "Then intrigue. We had to learn to trust one another. Now we're heading to the getting-to-know-one-another portion of the relationship."

Zoe rested her head on her hand. "Don't you think we went about this backward?"

Ben understood her need for order, but he shook his head. "You play the hand you're dealt," he told her. "I like your hair like this."

She'd let the curls stay loose and wild. "I know—that's why I left it down. I want you to be happy."

"You're going to have to go back to work sometime soon."

"I will. I feel bad about you getting shot over me." She kissed his neck and under his chin, moving up to his lips.

"If I had to get shot, I would want you as my reward every time." Ben looked into her eyes. "This is what I do. I save people from bad guys. There's not always this level of danger, Zoe."

"You're not going to stop?"

Ben shook his head. He couldn't imagine doing anything else. "I love you for caring about me. But I'll take extra care in making sure I come home in one piece."

She put her forehead on his breastbone. "You're always going to do the right thing?"

Besides being beautiful there was this sense of justice about her that he admired and made his work all the more important. He wanted her so badly, but he needed her to understand what he did was important, too. "Always, Zoe."

She wrapped her arms around his waist and held him with her whole body. He had never felt more in love.

"Darling, I love you," she said. "I want us to be together and I don't want to be afraid. When you're better I want us to go away so that we can really get to know one another."

"I like that idea," he said, beginning to strip off her clothes.

"Ben," she purred, unbuttoning his shirt and gingerly sliding it off his arm, "do we have too much sex?"

He looked down at her and knew he'd never loved like this before. "There's no such thing, baby. I love you, Zoe."

She cupped his face and sighed when he entered her. "I love you, Ben, and I'm not going anywhere."

Ben's heart had heard her and he knew he'd found the most perfect solitaire, his most perfect woman in the world.

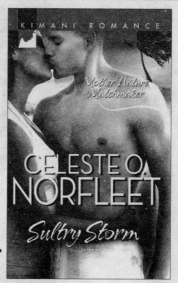

REQUEST YOUR FREE BOOKS!

2 FREE NOVELS
PLUS 2 FREE GIFTS!

KIMANI ROMANCE™

Love's ultimate destination!

KROM09